WALL OF DARKNESS

ISBN-10: 1-58790-020-3 / ISBN-13: 978-1-58790-020-4 / 126 pages / paperback / $14.95

This novel takes a hard look at cults that kill. Based upon real accounts of runaway teens, the story about a group of pedophiles is set in a garden paradise in Hawaii and depicts an investigation of the etiology of sex on the Internet to exploit vulnerable children.

A psychological profiler of extensive expertise, the author writes from her work in the trenches of cyber crime.
—William B. Sloan, Attorney

Teenage Violence — a whole new planet.
— James Delessandro, script doctor, author *Bohemian Heart*

THE ETERNITY LOOK

ISBN-10: 1-58790-052-1 / ISBN-13: 978-1-58790-052-5 / 231 pages / paperback / $14.95

A whodunit introducing U.S. Marshal Dalton Keys who staffs high security prison wards and tracks down clandestine drug manufacturers. Keys goes after a bonemaster paper manufacturer whose vendetta begins with the deaths of a captain who provided tactics and deployment and his disabled son in a pool of kaolin and cyanide.

A convincing plot, attractive protagonist and winning prose.
— Publishers Weekly

Reliably mystifying. A pro book from a pro tracker who goes with the detectives on beat patrol and into the field with the sheriff coroner. — SISTERS IN CRIME, San Rafael

DOMINO

ISBN-10: 1-58790-068-8 / ISBN-13: 978-1-58790-068-6 / 238 pages / paperback / $14.95

In this second Dalton Keys thriller, U.S. Marshal Keys sets out to avenge a fellow officer who is killed in the line of duty. Isaiah Du Bois is the first African American gay cop to be reassigned to highway 395 after an inner city corruption case in a police department blows sky high.

Exhaustive descriptions of locale and detailed analysis.
— MYSTERY COLUMN, Rex E. Klett

THE SWEAT BOX

ISBN-10: 1-58790-106-4 / ISBN-13: 978-1-58790-106-5 / 216 pages / paperback / $16.95

A series of unsavory acts ties a rancher in Texas to old farming money in California. In this third Dalton Keys mystery, U.S. Marshal Keys wends his way through an entanglement of relationships to corner a barn burner and killer.

> *A fast-paced whodunit — you never know what to expect next.*
> — SACRAMENTO MYSTERY READERS

UNDER DRAGON HOUSE

ISBN-10: 1-58790-090-4 / ISBN-13: 978-1-58790-090-7 / 238 pages / paperback / $14.95

This fourth Dalton Keys mystery finds the illegal sale of firearms to insurgents leading to a statewide manhunt for the son of a priest turned tracker. Addie Marjoe has all the makings of a maverick cop except he's his own dungeon keeper in this novel on customs and abortion rights.

> *Full of complex, twisty suspense.*
> — David Doerrer, MYSTERY SCENE

BLUEPRINT

ISBN-10: 1-58790-157-9 / ISBN-13: 978-1-58790-157-7 / 170 pages / paperback / $22

Fifth and last Dalton Keys based on the actual 1951 New York subway bombing, leads to a suspected reunion of terrorists who commit a mine bombing in the California desert.

> *An excellent, well-portrayed loot book, fast paced, gripping action.*
> — MYSTERIES IN BRIEF

SNAPSHOT, COLLECTED STORIES

ISBN-10: 1-58790-158-4 / ISBN-13: 978-1-58790-158-4 / 170 pages / paperback / $20

A collection of compassionately told stories that include eight short works previously published in Ellery Queen Mystery Magazine under the author's pen name Lea Cash-Domingo.

> *Consistently superb, substantive well-crafted puzzlers.*
> — Library Journal

> *One of the most notable features of Judy Koretsky's stories is the vivid depiction of setting. Judy brings her background so thoroughly to life that she seems to create a painting with words.*
> —ELLERY QUEEN MYSTERY MAGAZINE

CHERISHED MEMORY, POEMS & A PLAY

ISBN-10: 1-58790-152-8 / ISBN-13: 978-1-58790-152-2 / 92 pages / paperback / $18

Written in the style of Shakespearean sonnets, there are over two hundred poems in this book. This is Ms. Koretsky's first work of poetry. "How many days will it take to know you?/ When sweet designs their answers echo clear?/ Once agreed will you tumble fast and true/ And hold me close and always keep me near?/ Or will you fickle for sweet restraint/ Fall for some other woman's arduous complaint?"

ROPE

ISBN-10: 1-58790-171-4 / ISBN-13: 978-1-58790-171-3 / 344 pages / paperback / $27

Three novels-in-one book also featuring ROOM and DEATH-MASK each about Criminal Intelligence Division investigations in Scotland and England. In ROPE three physicians-in-training and five nurse shipmates are murdered by rope hanging at their college of medicine in Edinburgh, Scotland after a day outing consisting of military exercises. In ROOM the controversial "no egg" case focuses on a team of divers whose bodies were found in opaque morgue bags after a locked room shooting death of a county planning commissioner. In DEATHMASK the famous Brughel murder of a young Backwalk girl who is brutally stabbed haunts forensic detectives in the Clough in Ireland.

A must read for mystery and suspense buffs.

— Library Journal

The camera's eye is almost never shut — the fiction journalist who's been everywhere wants a clear and convincing byline. When triage finds another DOA in the water, you are right there as expert witness. — MURDER & MAYHEM, Marin

Barnes & Noble gives ROPE a five star rating.

Tower Books ranks ROPE #1 in Fantasy-Historical

TROJAN PARK

TROJAN PARK

A CALIFORNIA MYSTERY

J. LEA KORETSKY

REGENT PRESS
BERKELEY, CA

ISBN 13: 978-1-587890-211-6
ISBN 10: 1-58790-211-7
Library of Congress Control Number: 2010936067

The characters and events in this book are ficticious. Any reference to an actual place, any similarity to real people, living or dead, is entirely coincidental and not intended by the author.

10 9 8 7 6 5 4 3 2 1

Back Cover portrait of the author by G. Paul Bishop, Jr.
www.gpaulbishop.com

Front Cover photograph of the de Jung Museum
by George Auzans (GShotFoto)

Manufactured in the U.S.A.

REGENT PRESS
2747 Regent Street
Berkeley, CA 94705
www.regentpress.net

CHAPTER 1. OAKLAND

THE TRAIN CLAMORED through the brush, faint russet fields flickering with the dimming sunlight. A glimpse of a red barn momentarily showed through. Freshwater ponds, big squares of water, fell alongside a stretch of trimmed wheat as the train angled around a bend and shot past a Christmas tree forest. The air was sharply clear as the unexpected popped onto an ever changing landscape. The sunlight at two in an afternoon that resembled four-thirty on a winter day took in aspen pole trees with pointed tops darting dramatically into view, patches of water one instant squares seen in the distance, the next stark like walls. A farmer on a small tractor was slowly tilling a field in this isolated river landscape. There was a primordial quality when the traveler's mind knew it had joined with the infinite and could outdistance the tremulous nature of life.

I worked an investigative bench for the county district attorney where I had met the man I married. He was one of seven attorneys who prosecuted my cases. I matched the trend of investigators who gave testimony for their field research, always dressed in tailored suits, usually a navy box pleat and navy long suit coat, a strand of pearls, low pumps. I was five feet nine, Caucasian, Russian descent, with a trim page boy, darkly brown hair, almond shaped eyes, wide in the mouth, slender boned, a pair of eyeglasses around my neck, a shoulder holster, a tin of resin for my fingertips so that when I took the witness stand I could easily flip through the pages of the voluminous documents of witness exhibits. The court calendar took most of my time; evening and night hours were spent performing surveillance, working security, occasionally interviewing an inmate at a jail, or meeting a family and obtaining information which would subsequently be used in the Family Law, Probation, or Criminal courts.

I was thinking as rain pummelled grassy fields that despite my achievements, age, the lessons of life, I was nevertheless dissatisfied. I had at age fifty-seven, a middle-aged female of some repute, arrived to believe I might enjoy a wholly different set of accomplishments — that I had embarked on a journey for selfhood, to redefine my personhood, stretching inward for something perceived, though not yet realized, as I doggedly pursued new self definitions. I had divorced late in life at forty-five after being married for 11 years and some odd months, and in the process of separation and of discovering myself burdened with remembrances and possessions, I had met John and attempted to exchange a rather bleak life for instant newness.

Pain makes one irritable and self-conscious. I had surprisingly found myself upset with my new married life, hemmed in and unsupported, living too far from my job, facing an hour commute from Alameda that put me on the highway late. Yet once I overcame my guilt at having put him off temporarily, I felt cut adrift, purposeless, and without a definition of where I had come to. I had gone through a troubling four years during which I caused arguments with my closest friends and not surprisingly they eventually found their ways to better, less conflicted friends; even my employer who I trusted and had hoped would see me as a lifelong friend became angered and pushed me away pulling me off rotation and relegating me to lonesome assignments and even lonelier, more dismal investigations.

After two years of therapy examining my reasons for alienating my close friends, at making myself miserable; after fleeing the pain of separation, the loss of an image of a beloved, after traveling to nearly every national campground in seven western states, and keeping a journal, which in a moment of depression I threw away, I arrived. The point of arrival is to know after time has passed one is still waiting. The life I thought would be the one I claimed was now not even a remote possibility. There were many choices, but none seemed fulfilling, even worse, when I readied myself to act upon any or one, I found my mood apathetic, dulled. And so I had come to find myself too self absorbed, too closed in, not far reaching by any stretch of the imagination, feeling defeated by setbacks — a failed investigation with no conclusion but with the perpetrators by now a happy set of townhouse owners in Seattle, being passed over for promotion, six rejections from other potential posts, my son Marion who once thought I could do no wrong now encouraging but looking elsewhere for an adult role model, life just not being right.

I was traveling from Marion's home in Prescott on the Columbia River Highway. He was lucky. Marion had had time in his busy scientific schedule, between teaching classes in Portland and studying database designs for the law firm he worked for, to take me to the observatory to his office and laboratory and I had discovered what drove him as I rarely felt in the twenty-one years I had raised him.

Cows grazed, legs deep in the soggy marshland. This was a soil which when it rained there was nowhere for the water to go. It would pool on the soil saturating it. Moss-laden mountains were sided by rich dark shale scaling a hundred feet and by pockets of kelly green fern and by shaggy redwood trees. The day was overcast, cold and wet. The train moved through wildberry bushes and bare treacherous groves, through stagnant insect glazed ponds, past long barns, brown shingle one-room cottages, past a small harbor with a jetty of rocks and a pier with fishing boats with pulleys on them and boats coming in at two knots an hour.

By the time I had disembarked at Jack London Square and picked up the car rental, it was nightfall. The warm sultry hour gave me an illusion of being carefree. The reality was I had a week before I had to return to my desk and tackle the twenty cases to find the details that could crack the case I'd gone on vacation for. I headed for the freeway and for the garden estate of my one-time criminology partner.

Terry Roark's place was high enough to look down on Oakland's Pill Hill with its slab-like hospitals lit occasionally by red warnings of ambulances. The doorman took my jacket and disappeared behind the Miro painting. In a wall mirror I glanced at myself: a thin babe with shoulder length hair cashing in on what was once an ebullient downhill skier, dressed in jeans and a plaid grey and white shirt, greenish blue eyes and a dark expression. In the living room a few dozen people stood around drinking and talking. I took in the decor: Terry had finally discarded the Venus statues with their offbeat snorkels and sashes. In their places were elaborately carved antique tables with beautiful birds of paradise flowers arranged in tall ebony vases.

In the corner an elderly African American man with silver hair was playing a baby grand piano as a white woman in a sequined fire engine red gown belted out a tune from Porgy and Bess, her mane of kinky red hair shaking energetically.

The piano player ended the tune on a lonesome note. As I made my way toward the patio, he cracked a smile.

"Hey there, Cutie." He grinned out of the side of his mouth.

"Nice tune," I said, and gave a boyish look typical of the Oakland crowd I worked with. Seeing Terry, I tried to extricate myself but the piano player tugged at me.

"C'mon sweet thing, come dance with me," the singer said, and winked as the piano player stepped into a jazz number.

"You don't remember but you saw me half a dozen times when you worked in the city," she said. "You and Terry were at the gallery where I was singing bee-bop." She flashed me her perfect pearly whites.

I remembered her. Life was kinder in those days to us all. She was a young twenty in a flashy white sports car who waved to whichever group of students clustered at the stairs to a mansion on Van Ness where new criminologists congregated with equally new attorneys.

She said, "We dance for twenty years and sleep for a hundred. You an attorney?"

"D.A."

"That's nice. I knew straight away you were another attorney. You doing security here, or what?"

"Neither. I'm a guest. And you? You handle nightclub acts?"

"No longer. Too much publicity."

I couldn't imagine her having a private life. Too much glitter, too much eccentricity.

"Hey, baby," a lanky man with expensive tweeds and black hair slicked behind his ears draped an affectionate arm around her hefty waist. "Gonna sing me another?"

"Sure, sugar, all night long." She reached inside his breast pocket for a cigarette and lit it.

"Carole," the piano player tapped his watch.

I hightailed it into the other room. The woman reminded me of my first clients when I was doing my first year internship for a small firm tracking missing accounts. I was an idealistic greenhorn with dreams of rising up a corporate hierarchy, but after a few years in medical records at the Presidio, the hope died an instant death. I'd seen enough stupidity — bad bedside manners, failure to obtain a thorough medical history, wrong X-rays, mistaken lab results, and a zillion lawsuits.

I drifted into the garden. A small crowd of ten had gathered near the rock fountain. A uniformed waiter carried glasses of champagne, and I took one. Dark pink bougainvillea stood out against a retaining wall that surrounded the property.

I saw Terry, a glass of champagne in her hand. She wore a pastel green silk dress that left one shoulder bare. The green suited her lightly tan complexion, brown eyes and shoulder length wavy brown hair.

Terry's husband Wesley Roark, a local millionaire out of Austin, Texas, had after their divorce left her with this house and a summer home on the beach at Half Moon Bay.

"There you are," she said. She took my hand and gave me a kiss. "I'm glad you made it. I see Carole monopolized you."

"It was painless," to which she produced a broad smile, all lips. "How's the new love of your life?"

"Albert is fine. He was in surgery this morning performing an emergency appendectomy and tonight with an ectopic."

"Risky business, tubal pregnancies."

"No kidding. I thank my lucky stars not to ever have had a problem like that."

"Is Albert gone much?"

"As much as Wes was. I'm lucky if I see him one night a week."

"And you? Are you still working with The Roark Museum?"

"I stopped that years ago after Wes remarried. That position is the caveat he offers his wives. Every now and then if I come across a property I like, I'll ask Wes if he's interested but he generally defers to Geneva."

"You seem younger, if that's possible."

"Long hours spent sunning on the lawn. We are groomed for idle time."

She steered me by the elbow inside the long modern, all glass home into the well-lit hall. "Let's duck into the study so we can talk while I'm alert enough to think clearly."

"Is this the matter you referred to on the phone yesterday?" I asked.

"It is. It's a real stickler. The worst of this is I have to put on a show and pretend my life is more or less in order even though it isn't."

"Trouble with Randall?"

Two brown tweed couches faced a twenty-four inch television screen. Pictures of Terry and her now seventeen year old son Randall decorated the walls. Terry closed the door on muffled laughter and sat with me on the sofa.

"I'm being blackmailed. I believe Randall is behind it."

"That's pretty extreme."

"He has very expensive tastes without the necessary financial means to provide for them. Most adolescents his age drive jeeps, Chevrolets or station wagons or Stanzas or Kias — Randall, he has a red Corvette with white walls. He wears Gucci shoes or Mock toes, tweed jackets, silk ties. Even I don't dress up every day."

She fumbled with a cigarette from a silver box on the table and handed me one which she lit with a gold butane lighter, her hand trembling slightly. "Jesus, I'm a nervous wreck. I guess I'm not made of steel as I thought I was."

"What leads you to believe it's Randall?"

"I received a note in which I was instructed to prepare a hundred thousand from two banks. Well, one is his account established by Wes and the other is mine."

"Did you make a copy of the note?"

"No, I burned it. I was afraid someone would find it and ask me about it."

"And you believe the information as to your bank accounts is not common knowledge?"

"I suppose my son's friends might know about these accounts although it is extremely unlikely."

"Did the demand list the actual account numbers?"

"Yes, that's what's so odd."

"Did you follow the instructions?"

"Yes, I wired the money from those accounts to a number listed on the note."

"Did you receive confirmation from the receiving bank?"

"I attempted to but was unsuccessful."

"Why do you think your son is capable of such a demand?"

"I don't know that he is. It's just why would the person ask for our family accounts?"

"Seems to me this could be anyone," I said, considering all possibilities. "When did you last see your son?"

"A week ago Sunday here. He was argumentative, intimidating but then he has behaved this way for the past year. It's possible he's experimenting with drugs." A twinge of disdain lived in her tone.

She continued with, "He flunked his first semester in his senior year. The principal asked Randall to repeat the semester and Randall all but threatened to paint the school yard red. I asked Albert to go with me to Wes's to speak to Randall but Randall wasn't there. We checked several of his friends but no one's heard from him. I thought I knew everything about him. Obviously I don't."

"That doesn't necessarily mean he's fallen in with a bad crowd. It's normal for affluent teen boys to try to bust loose at this age."

"Randall indicated he had a girlfriend and a studio apartment."

"Do you know where this place is located?"

"It's in Canyon, near the ranger station. I followed him once after we had a fight. It's very wooded there, very rural."

"How did Randall meet the girl?"

"I have no idea, even less how he covers rent. The landlord says he's been paying five hundred for nearly a half year. That means that since age sixteen he's been keeping this young woman."

"It's possible she's keeping him. These things do happen." I laid a reassuring hand on her arm. "How about if I check out a few things and get back to you?"

She gave a nod. "Just don't tell Wesley. I don't want him to learn of this."

"I can't very well not talk to him, Terry. A man in his position has a right to know and he may already know about the studio."

"I wish you wouldn't. He's been ill lately, and I'm concerned knowledge of this will be a strain on him."

"What about talking to his second wife? Geneva. What's her last name?"

"Genieve Canber. No, absolutely not."

"Could she be part of the reason Randall moved out?"

"I don't want to be blamed for attempting to stir things up, but she might be."

"How well do you get along with her?"

"I've met her a handful of times. We are very different, she and I. I can understand if Randall feels he doesn't belong there."

"Does he still sleep in his room?"

"From time to time, but it's rare."

"Okay, I'll see what I can do. If I need to reach you, do you have a private line where I can reach you?"

Some teens reached adulthood faster than others. I had become a mother when motherhood was viewed as a handicap in law enforcement because of the types of death threats dangerous cases often made. An unruly child could make home life hell and an obedient one could make a mediocre parent feel gifted. I'd been a mediocre parent by default, leaving my previous partner alone with Marion while I dealt with complicated cases which left no time even for sleep.

One couldn't beat the clock. The nesting instinct was strongest and many young men left home before they completed high school.

I'd known Randall as a child. The Roarks made up three generations of powerful and influential society, and Randall was an only child who but for Terry's wavy hair was his father's look alike. Randall was expected by age nineteen to follow into the family industry networks. Perhaps Randall had in glimpsing a look at himself in the mirror one day recoiled from the image of the man he was turning into and packed those dreams on the shelf in favor of giving himself a more basic identity of manhood and fatherhood.

I disregarded Terry's caution about not contacting Wesley Roark. Sooner or later the truth was bound to come out and I didn't want this man to feel secrets were being kept. Plus I thought I understood him. Although stern and emotionally remote, he had attended every parent/teacher conference while his son was in grammar school, had taken time from a burdensome schedule to coach his son's soccer practice, and had attempted to indoctrinate his son with a sense of the world by sending him to his extended family in London during summers. The more he did for his son, the more Randall seemed to retreat. I thought it was possible the young man needed his father with him more of the time.

The Roark estate was one of two properties on Parnassus Court. A circular drive fronted an imposing colonial mansion similar in style to antebellum homes. Marble stairs led to an elaborate parthenon entrance of miniature carved statues of draped nude females. Iron grillwork covered a circular window. A stately black and gold Packard stood in the drive. Behind it was a Silver Ghost. On either side of the home stood Tuscany trees in single file hiding an expansive acreage of five acres.

Wes was sole proprietor of the Roark Museum of Modern Art in San Francisco in Golden Gate Park. He had just acquired Bank of the East and resituated it on the ground floor of his six story glass extravaganza in which the museum was housed on the top three floors. Most museums were owned by the county or state or by a university, but Wesley Roark's backing was derived from some twenty thousand acres of forested land on the coast from Ukiah to Crescent City. The building was fronted by a waterfall and pool which spilled over six aquamarine copper frames at discordant angles to a bottom of gold coins. A long thin panel of icy blue glass on the side of the building revealed an elevator. The roof, resplendent crystal that formed an apex rose fifty feet above the gallery it covered, in radiant sunlight could be seen from the ocean sparkling like a jewel behind the

Sutro baths. At night the apex glowed ruby red. Wes was said to have paid a hefty ten million to have the building constructed, bringing in an artistic lineup of abstracts for security orientation to the interior, and the money was well-spent.

The door was opened by a uniformed maid.

"Lennis Cliford," I said, handing her my card.

"Come this way, please."

She led me across a marble tiled foyer into a drawing room, where she left me to wait. Its cool apricot tones gave the room a tranquil luminescence. The morning sunlight fell in wide streaks across a walnut desk and law bookshelves crammed full.

"Lenn, nice to see you," Wes Roark said.

He was as I remembered him: commanding with a stately presence. Greyish curly hair framed a chiseled worn expression. He wore silk green trousers, a stiff white shirt and a light green sweater vest with a pocket watch and chain.

The last time I had come to the house was on a burglary case. That case began with a party in the Oakland Hills at the home of Wes's first partner Jack Haner. Haner had gone the way of corporate attorneys with a focus on San Francisco corporate financial firms, as I was undertaking a criminalistics internship for San Francisco County after a brief stint in missing persons in San Mateo and then an even briefer study with the Department of Justice in Los Angeles conducting security clearances for top level bureaucratic executives. Nine years into corporate practice with a firm called Abraham and Sons, Inc. when Terry changed her venue, left a relationship with a high school sweetheart destined to be a surgeon, and within less than a year, to everyone's surprise, married Wes and became a mother, Haner had invented a fail-safe system for Wes Roark.

I said, "This is not meant to be a social call, Sir."

"Come, come, Lenni, we're friends." He instructed me to sit, and we sat facing one another. "No need to address me with such civility. After all you are not a stranger," and smiled to make me feel at ease. "It's about Randall, is it? Did Terry tell you about our difficulties?"

"Terry asked me specifically not to bother you with this."

"I've had some pressures of late. I returned home late, it was after dark, and my valet was not at his post. I was met on the gravel by a young woman with a toddler who claimed she was my son's wife. She was dark with dark hair and she said Randall had run out on her and she could not afford to meet costs. I invited her inside. I realize I should've called the police to detain the boy the minute I saw him."

"Does the child resemble Randall?"

"His image identically. I wrote the young woman a check for two thousand dollars and asked her to send me information as to her particulars but I never heard a word since."

"Did you ask for identifying information?"

"I did. But she said she'd lost her purse and she had no driver's license."

I removed a pencil and a spiral bound pad from my shirt pocket and flipped it open to a blank page. "Let's give this a shot. She's what? Bony in the face? Broad?"

"Dainty nose, dark eyes close together, small lips, black curly hair obscuring her forehead — -"

"Like this?" I showed him.

"That's quite good. Yes. Cheekbones a bit more pronounced." He watched as I sketched a likeness. "There!" when the drawing matched the likeness. "That's her. She said her name was Roberta Klee."

I jotted down the spelling. "Is the name pronounced Clay?"

"Yes. She said the child was three and that she'd named him Terence. I jumped to the conclusion that Randall wanted him named that and am afraid I asked without thinking if she'd named him after my father to which she replied she'd had the child out of wedlock."

"Are you aware that Terry followed Randall to a wooded secluded house in Canyon where she saw this young woman?"

His face registered surprise. "No, I had no idea, but then

we don't communicate much. Is Randall alright?"

"Terry believes he may be responsible for blackmailing her. She received a demand note for a hundred thousand dollars which she complied with."

"That's a staggering amount of money. It can't possibly be Randall doing that."

"Do you give him an allowance?"

"He has a bank account. At any given time I put a few hundred a month into it."

"Any idea what he does with the money?"

"It never crossed my mind to ask him."

"Does your son have enemies?"

"Everyone has enemies. I'm just not aware of who these people might be for him. Two years ago Randall won a marathon running race at a boarding school in London and there were a handful of competitors."

"Do you have the names of those individuals?"

"It'd be no trouble to get you the yearbook with that information."

"Could this young lady be someone he met when he was in London?"

"I hadn't thought of that. Yes, that would be a logical explanation for all this."

"Can you provide me with your son's date of birth, his vehicle registration and license, school address and names and numbers of friends?"

"Certainly. I will put a packet together."

"Thank you."

I moved to the window overlooking the garden. A brick patio and strip of grass with garden chairs faced rows of flowers of every imaginable type — yellows, marigolds, daisies, iris, gladioli, interspersed with ferns, oleander trees, cactus and red leaf maple trees to a tennis court, which the wire fence was visible. A gardener's skillful hand was obviously at work. Each arrangement blended in for overall order and complementarity.

"Here we are." Wes Roark's voice called my attention. He gave me a manila envelope containing a thick yearbook. "Good seeing you again, do call as soon as you know anything, won't you?"

I said I would.

As I pulled out of the drive, Roark stood, hands in his pockets, looking less like a man in control of millions than a man who may have lost a trusted relationship with the most important individual in his life.

CHAPTER 2.

SAN FRANCISCO IS A SEASCAPE of mansions on its ocean side, an avenue of colorful Victorians on Potrero Hill and closest to the Bay Bridge a lineup of warehouses and engineering offices. On Treasure Island is an airport tower and below lies the flattest land anyone with experience of landfill will tell you. As you stand on it, the bay stretches out as a rough carpet and the Golden Gate Bridge directly ahead rising behind the prison, one's gaze catches Nob Hill perched on the city's shoulder with half a dozen piers and ships evident.

Sometime around 1957 the city built rows upon rows of ticky tacky single family dwellings which covered the barren earth from Potrero Hill to the Cow Palace. Real estate was a boon for a good thirty years and hammer and nail socked a pretty good punch in and around City Hall and government offices. Brochures were responsible for bringing the new European continent to prosperity. With it emerged a concept of the twenty-first century, the idea that the buying and selling of information could lead to great things, to new genteel communities, more banks, more services. There was the creation of religious and ethnic communities, enhanced financial postures that gave way to block long synagogues or churches or to educational institutions, foundations, parks, monuments, middle class flats and ghettos — Chinese, Buddhist, French, Majorcan and so on.

After my parents divorced when I was seventeen, I left Oakland to live for a handful of years in San Francisco with my uncle who served in the military at the Presidio. We resided in officer housing, then moved off the base to Brisbane out near the airport. It was my final year in high school and apart from a healthy circle of military brats and suburban yids, I prepared for midterm and final exams in study halls with

European debutantes and young women whose parents were architects of mansions and cities. From time to time there were rites of passage and lavish parties in rented halls to celebrate the end of one's studious years and entrance to academia and a career post.

It is not possible to come of age in a community where professionalism outranks any other ambition without becoming largely influenced by that community. After my father returned to live with his new bride in Berkeley, I, faced with friends leaving for eastern seaboard colleges, submitted to two years as an undergraduate to medical school curriculum at the University of San Francisco, a private institution.

The proximity to the Chinese and Laotian community kept me in their antique shops, part of a captive audience who would learn to buy and sell commodities, among them diamonds, opals, citron, not to mention transistors, cameras and CDs, for television. The introduction to computer forensics took me to a frontier which at eighteen I understood little of, but which the Asians had immediate access to in their global technologies including e-fax machines, internet and laser imprints. A dollar was a dollar, its counterfeit counterpart exposed when medical technology brought enhancements into the picture. Language translations, hieroglyphics for ancient artifacts and coin, sound devices to interpret alarm codes and safes all became accessible by simply plugging into the outlet which was automatically monitored by PG&E and computer memory. Computer text was emptied at whim, splashed into a big pond and sold to bidders seeking information for books, magazines, television, anything. This was the information network flowing like blood into the arteries of government and private sector to domestic networks and Wall Street as well as to unseen enemy agents. The buying and selling of information was instantaneous, and was the single most sought-after commodity in the global marketplace.

The Cold War was over, securely tucked behind a facade of growth. National brokering into commodity banks was also diminishing, replaced by tough, no-nonsense systems which provided layer upon layer of bricks which when penetrated led to another maze, another system, another universe. The worst of it for Americans was the over utilization of her forests, the shrinking of her cubic feet of usable water, endless tapping of mineral resources, a predictable glut of her currency not to mention saddling her ships and production to stillborn ports in foreign governments where housing was rapidly leading to destitute overpopulation. The story myth of Paul Bunyan was gone; the age of forestry as an unconquerable territory also gone, and with it the dizzying speed of an endless mesh of freeways, highrises, cars and city lights.

The home in Canyon stood at the end of a dirt road. It was small, a one bedroom cottage with a veranda. I knocked at the door but no one answered. I tried the latch and finding it unlocked, entered.

The interior was dark, depressed. A single bed sat against one wall like a sofa with throw pillows. A crib and stuffed arm-chair faced a fireplace which looked as if it hadn't been lit in years. A hall led to a small kitchen with a stove and refrigerator and restroom with a closet. It was neat, sparse and compact. The cupboards were mostly bare except for some glasses and plates. Inside the refrigerator was a tin with refried beans and beef with mole sauce, a carton of eggs, a bottle of milk that read Berkeley Farms, and a pack of mentholated Cool cigarettes.

Not much, if this was all one had to live for.

I returned to the sitting room and waited in the armchair for the resident. Some forty minutes later, the door pushed open.

"Jesus, Lenn, you scared the crap out of me!" Randall said, as he set down a cardboard box filled with groceries on the counter.

I sized up the young man. He had put on some weight since I had last seen him. His face was filled out, his red kinky hair stood out like an afro. He wore sturdy blue jeans, a cotton navy turtleneck and a navy and white checkered flannel shirt, with boots. "Your mother asked me to look in on you."

"We had a fight and I haven't gone back to apologize."

"Your father said a friend of yours showed up at the house."

"Which friend?"

"A woman with a child."

Randall smiled. "That's my wife and child. I'm a father now."

"Teen parenthood is a rough call for anyone."

"Yeah, well, I'm alright with it. We'll make out okay. It's better than getting in people's way and being made to feel like a butt for it."

"I gathered. Your dad didn't realize you'd moved out."

"Well, I haven't actually made up my mind about it yet. I'm at home a few days a week."

I helped myself to a strip of beef jerky. "Given any thought to running your dad's office?"

"I abdicated. He's not interested and neither am I."

"How do you know? Maybe you should give it a try. Sure beats raising a child and wife in a log cabin."

"That's your opinion. I think I'm doing fine. I'm pumping gas weekends and working in a grocery store nights."

"But you don't have to. Your whole life is waiting for you at home."

"But I ought to have a say at this. After all it is my life."

"You're too young to be able to choose wisely."

"I have people who need me. Janie needs me. I'm a good father."

"Janie? I thought her name was Roberta Klee?"

"No, it's Jane. Roberta's someone else."

"Jane what?"

"Hart," he answered with a strong undercurrent of resentment.

"Does Jane drive? Have a separate address?"

"Look, Lenn, I'm not giving you the third degree. She's my wife, okay? That should be enough for you."

I backed down, in order not to antagonize the young man's determination. "Janie, it seems, asked your dad for money."

"She shouldn't have done that. I'll have to ask her about that. You can tell my mother I'm okay. I don't need her money, or anything else."

"You like this guy she's living with?"

"Albert? I guess so. He's nice to her when he's there."

"He's not home much, is he?"

"No, he isn't." He smiled, as if to suggest an irony that his father was the same way. "I know I seem young to you, that I'm — "

"I'm scared for you is all," I cut in. "You aren't old enough to begin to understand what you're up against."

"I'm okay, really. I'll go home and see my dad this week, okay?"

"Sure."

Randall put the perishables in the refrigerator. He stocked dried and canned goods onto the bare shelves and stashed the nuts and dried fruits into a bin. "I'm going to can fruit this summer," he said, and proudly opened a cabinet to show off dozens of mason jars with tops. "I've got some other ideas. I thought I'd try my hand at fiberglass manufacture and make swimming pool covers."

"Great idea. So where's this wife of yours?"

"Oh she won't show as long as there's a strange jeep parked outside."

"You want me to hide it?"

"No." He removed a cigarette and offered me one. Lighting them, Randall spoke with the cigarette between his teeth, "She has a record for which she did time. She just doesn't like cops."

I eyed him. According to the older Roark's version, Janie wasn't much older than Randall. "How old is Janie?"

"She's twenty-eight."

"Could qualify as statutory rape, young man," to which

Randall Roark gave me a weary look that said he was about to crack under the strain of his father's rejection. "You want to tell me about it?"

"My dad hates me."

"No, he doesn't."

"We're at the go figure stage," he replied, his voice strained. "I ask a question and he says, sit down, take a breath and think about it. Then I tell him I'm thinking and nothing's coming and he says I need to think longer until something comes. I guess I'm a disappointment."

"He wants you to be self-sufficient."

"I am."

"Are you blackmailing your mother?"

Randall coughed on his cigarette. "Jesus! What kind of question is that?"

"Someone wanted a hundred thousand dollars from hers and your accounts."

"That's a huge amount of money."

"Those were your father's exact words."

"No, I'm not. That wouldn't even occur to me." And then he heaved. "You believe me, don't you?"

I wasn't sure. From the surface it looked as though Randall were the only one with a motive. "Let's keep in touch, okay?"

"I haven't got a phone."

I laid out two dollars worth of quarters and dimes with a business card. "Need bus money too?"

"No, I got the idea."

Whatever degree of fight in him, he was still seventeen. And at seventeen, despite their belief that any obstacle could be challenged and defeated, they could not adequately provide for themselves without adult support.

I was unable to trace the bank wire, but a check had been written against a corporation in southern California. I tried a number of prefixes on my computer and came up with a lead. From the looks of it, the receiver had set up a time limited account in order to receive the check and then shut down operations. I turned the detail over to a programming specialist.

Then I ran a clearance on Randall's vehicle registration. A replacement vehicle provided by the insurance also turned up missing within a few days. Randall had purchased a Chevrolet loaner off an auto lot for two hundred and fifty dollars and registered it under the name, Sam Jackson. He paid cash for insurance on it. When his Corvette was finally located, it was found in King City with the radio ripped out. He brought it back and changed his name on the pink slip to Terence, the name of his child.

To top it off Jane Hart had a record — for passing bad checks and forgery.

All in all, I summed up the situation as a young man in serious trouble with the law, his family or some unidentified officer who was hell bent on giving this teenager a run for his money.

When the information came back on the account, it was for a man named Neil Holyer. I ran a make on the name in California and found a Holyer in east Oakland near Mills College.

CHAPTER 3.

IF THE HOME IS THE PRIVATE SANCTUARY for the soul, then Neil Holyer's two thousand square foot house on a small cul-de-sac bordered on all sides by oak trees and Spanish-style, copper doors, long sash window homes with fish ponds and Japanese lantern garden lights was just that.

"Mr. Holyer?"

"Pleased to finally have a person to put with a name, Ms. Cliford." He was tall, slender, blondish, dressed in light grey tweed pants and a white silk shirt with wingtip loafers.

"Likewise. I came across your name once in a fence job of stolen hologram seals filed on by Mr. Roark."

"Your name sticks out as indelible ink in my art dealings, you're the mirror-retrievable entry detective who works with Oakland police waterways."

"Yes. I've had my fair share of speedboat holdups."

Since I had been the deputy attorney to file on the burglary and had determined an accurate suspect on the foundation that the gate had been pried open cell-phone style, I was known to the owner for more than polite recorded interviews.

For Holyer his one story luxurious apartment was a rendition of dwellings in the Vieux Carre. The hall was long, the ash floors glistened, the ceilings were high, crammed bookshelves in the front room with a lone sofa from the Barbara Barry collection, the tables from Moorpark California, the drapes from Dumaine Inc. At age forty-eight Holyer had made none too many mistakes except he had traded in affordability for comfort. If continual sounds of a jet in flight plagued the Oakland skies, then the interior borrowed from a feeling of calm, of more than periodic Zen, justified by designer secrets.

We sat in a family room at the back of the house, Holyer at a desk where an anesthetized puppy lay, glass smashed in its paw, I on a checkered navy and yellow sofa. The floor was tiled, wooden beams ran across the ceiling, small red lights intertwined hung in the manifestation of chili peppers on the wall. The room overlooked a lawn and pool and was surrounded by a bronze tiled stone wall with a hedge. Above the fence through a mass of trees a two story house peered through, the suggestion of a balcony and lounge chairs.

"We're the disadvantaged upper middle class," Neil explained, lines of tension cropping around his eyes and mouth as he smiled, and resumed his task with a small cloth, rubbing alcohol and tweezers. "It used to be I owned invaluable art objects which periodically walked out of my backyard like a common farm pet. During one year I put in three calls to the police."

"Do you remember whom you talked to?"

"Sgt. Brice came out."

"On each occasion?"

"Two out of three times."

"And the third?"

"Officer Ames."

Brice handled missing art objects valued over five grand per item and Ames was on harassment. "The reason I ask is because I'm investigating any possibility of overlap as to Mr. Roark's son."

"I scarcely think he's the cause of my disappearing art."

"I'm just trying to verify information." I was aware of resistance in the other man, and said, to be placating in order to draw him out, "Randall appears to be a young man in need of rather a good sum of money. Has Mrs. Roark ever discussed this matter with you?"

Neil completed the removal of glass, saying as he spoke, "It wasn't quite that straightforward. He's living with a woman now, but six months ago he was the outcast in a family where the parents were continually at war. Terry would say Randall was sleeping all day, she couldn't get him out of bed, he sat at his father's pool all day — "

"Could Wes confirm that?"

"I certainly took him at his word." To the dog, "There, there, Simone, all fixed," and wrapped the paw in gauze, then popped a pill into her mouth. He placed the dog on a rug on the floor and settled onto a yellow leather easy chair. "Randall's life kept him at his father's night and day. I heard an earful from Wes now and then."

"What did he say?"

"He was upset his son wouldn't take summer jobs, forged his father's signature on checks, dipped into protected funds and gave them to God knows who, left the computer on all night, and took the car keys to the Silver Ghost roadster. Wes had me establish an account to track the money Randall was spending."

"I came across your account. That was a sizable check."

"Mistake or not, we didn't put it through. Randall told his father it was for his vehicle, so Wes wrote a check for that. Wes's instructions have been to pass through the checks in question and then hold the account closed temporarily."

"Was he worried about road accidents?"

"You know, you expect that with a kid who's stretching his loins, but the fact is I don't know. Wes's classic cars are in good shape as far as I know and the Corvette was fine until it was stolen. The problems for him have been with the hired help who've managed his automobile stables. My understanding is they weren't very reliable."

"Does he have trouble keeping good people?"

"Well he's rich, too visible and known commercially everywhere. He's infiltrated is what it is."

I changed the subject to his theft. "When Officer Ames came out, what had occurred here?"

Neil nodded appreciatively, "I had called it in as harassment. I had sold the joint lot, landscaped the yard as you see it and found the patio littered with wood scrap — "

"As if the pieces had come from next door?"

"That's what I thought. In fact I went next door and found

the home neat as a whistle. No stray parts anywhere, everything tacked down."

"Was that house built?"

"No, it was in process. The structure was completed and the kitchen walls were in but the second story had not yet been added. There was a pile of lumber."

"Did you receive a copy of Ames's report?"

"Yes. Do you want to see it?"

"If you have it on hand."

Holyer went to retrieve it from another room. When he returned, he handed me the report.

It was four pages including the summary written in the dry style that the police provide for their documentation of relevant events. No evidence was taken. The lieutenant supervising Ames closed the case. There was no mention of a referral to the FBI which often was a next step.

Holyer said, "I was struck though by the fact that these were pegs, if not rather large ones, which seemed to correspond to my way of thinking not with poor Randall but with my computer computations."

"What is it you do?"

"I handle objects of art for galleries. Until recently prior to it being torn down I brought in art for the DeYoung from many ports, China being one."

"Did Terry or Wes obtain their paintings through you?"

"Both." He laughed. "I purchase for their entire social circle. You know the piece in her living room where the piano is?"

I remembered it. The lightweight yellow opaque square plate with a red and black curlicue placed over the lower right corner of a red plate with an irregular yellow scrawl.

"I purchased that from the Stuart collection in Berlin. You probably didn't see it but Wes has a signature item from Belgium. It's translucent dark blue glass fronted by silver waves and metallic stamps inside a reflecting square. He paid twenty-five thousand for it. He had me purchase one four feet high for the Roark Museum. Before they married, Teresa managed all collection acquisitions. Yearly she selected different themes. The red moon, red sun material was the theme for 1985. In 1986 she focussed on predominantly Russian art although Wes reached for far more international symbolism."

"Well, I know Wes is British."

"To the core."

"And he assigns you collections he wishes to acquire?"

"Most of the time he tells me. On occasion I recommend."

"You must earn an enviable income."

"It fluctuates. Year to year is very little, although when I make a sale I can net twenty-five thousand to a hundred thousand." He paused, eyebrows furrowed. "Now that I think about it Wes has an associate in San Rafael whom Randall spent summer months with as a child who spared no expense on architecture, as Wes has done on a handful of collectibles."

"His name?"

"Hauptman."

"First name?"

"Mitchel. His litho prints are typically described in German according to paper type style and weight."

"As for a book?"

"Yes, every description of a collection item that is a print is registered in a ledger which is publicized in German as well as in English. It's possible Hauptman may have brought young Randall in."

"Or may have influenced him for a particular task. Where might I find Mitchel Hauptman?"

"Good question. After his son died he went into a funk and although this was a number of years ago, he hasn't done well over the years."

I waited for the explanation.

"The son's name was Knowles Hauptman. He was an artist of known repute. The mother owned a restaurant and nightclub called The Soundless Wave. You may have heard of it."

I hadn't. "How did Knowles die?"

"Knowles gashed his head in a state of drunkenness in the garden. His mother was the one who discovered him. She got up around midnight and went looking for him."

"What was he doing at his parents' home?"

"Going through a divorce. It's often the safest place to be."

To dodge in-law bullets, perhaps. "Who was the divorce from?"

"Genieve Canber, Wes' young wife. She married a Smith prior to her marriage to Hauptman. The first husband was a medical supplier who stocked a string of emergency rooms for private hospitals throughout California. Randall worked one summer as a patient billing clerk. Thereafter he was hired to manage accounts for Hauptman from time to time."

"Must've been quite an education for young Roark."

"His father wanted him at majority age for the museum acquisition collection. Apparently Randall had come up with a way to spot invaders in a database so that as you were working on a program if there were outside interference, a tracer could tag the source and eliminate access."

"For security purposes."

"Yes," with a quick nod. "Randall developed a very useful system."

"What types of properties are we talking about here? Art?"

"These are buildings, although as you know the Berlin diamond is on display. Alarm systems work on the premise that penetration can be targeted and identified. A museum is naturally going to have as good a security system as money can buy. Wes paid upward of three-quarters of million for his. It is made up of images which change shapes at various intervals and lock onto a pattern when invasion is evident. Also the scan device works the way the light in a lighthouse does, decoding in a three hundred and sixty degree radius. To penetrate his system one would need to be inside his system."

"Is it possible the wooden pegs you found in the yard were

in some way meant to tag your system, say by use of a photo, with the hope you would subsequently open your security system for review?"

"Officer Ames said that."

"What exactly did he say?"

"He felt I had done myself a disservice by selling the plot next door. He said it could be inferred based upon aerials taken by security that the architecture of my neighbor's home matched the pegs of the program that tests my system. He suggested I switch security firms, which is what I did."

"Who is your new firm?"

"Chalmer & Gaudde, on California Street. They have beefed up my systems with the protection I needed."

"One last question. Did Mr. Roark have a bank account accessible to you?"

"Yes, for acquisitions. One must for each block of transactions."

"Do you know anything about a blackmail demand?"

Neil perked up. "To whom? Wes?"

I nodded, to which he replied, "No, I did not."

I closed my notepad and pocketed it and my pen. "I want to thank you for your time. You have been very generous."

On the way out of the home my eye was drawn to the placement of sculpture in the hall and in adjoining rooms. It was either an interesting notion that to protect costly property a deliberate mechanism, a tag of some sort, had to be present inside the home in view of a window, perhaps as a way to determine whether a burglar had gained entry.

Officer Rick Ames remembered the case well.

Ames was classically Spaniard the way handsome men with European lines, chiseled face, a straight line nose, eyes evenly centered, skin light tan and cropped brown hair were viewed as enigmatic by the public they served. Although the police department strove in the seventies to bring in officers who physically matched the aestheticism of their changing demographics, by the year 2000 they were trying to draw experts in computer graphics who were also well practiced in forensics and courtroom testimony. Ames had beat the rest of the wolf hounds to the door, probably because in addition to the impressive rigamarole on his curriculum vitae, he had walked the mile in pulling bodies out of freezer boxes and preserving exotic slay beds in the mud.

"The situation was clear," Ames said. "I had the file which showed two break-ins into the garden, both for potentially pricey exhibit stuff. These had to have been known by the thief because there were other pieces readily accessible which according to our police consultant were equally as valuable but were never touched. Also these two pieces were cast by the same artist although there is some question as to authenticity of the second piece."

"And these pieces were actually in the garden?"

"Yes. There is a retaining wall, a virtually impenetrable wrought iron gate that locks from the inside and posts throughout the yard. My thought, and I still have reservations, was his gardener or maid service left open the gate."

"Any idea as to why?"

"No."

Instinct made me ask. "Anything to the museum?"

"Funny you should ask. We came across a date box, the kind the postal service gives to business owners. It was set for July 3, 2002 and all wires fed to the one date. We thought, it's a bomb but after we dumped it in a metal box it did not go off. We couldn't figure out what it was doing there. Maybe a detonation device wasn't inside it yet. But in taking it apart we found six wires each connected to a different slot and we decided this: it could take out a floor or a stairwell to a six story building as long as it didn't catch on fire as everything else will in a building that size."

"Perhaps that's why Wes put in a library and a bank."

"We considered that. The theft with the pegs was the tip. There were just too many pegs. That tells you right there that there are too many pictures, that the opera is governed by too many systems."

"Were there other similar thefts in your jurisdiction?"

"To the tycoon Wes Roark, to a restaurateur in Jack London Square named Francois LeValle, to a woman named Teresa D'Coteur — "

"You mean, the first Mrs. Roark?" I asked, surprised at the mention of her.

"Yes, and there was her brother."

"Who married an African woman from South San Francisco."

"Yes. All were in more or less the same social circle. Also a patron of the Roark Museum who resides in Half Moon Bay, a docent on Tamalpais and an administrator in Petaluma."

"Did this artist have other buyers?"

"Yes. He is well speculated. People have solicited his work from original buyers."

"Do you know by what methods? Do they frequent gallery showings for example?"

"You'd have to speak directly to the consultant."

"I'd like to."

Rick Ames wrote down the name and number.

"How did the concept of pictures arise?" I asked.

"It didn't, until I returned to the police lab and we asked the insurance firm for the photocopies of the works. The works were double paintings which when viewed from different angles showed a different painting.

"Black images on white background give no impression of distance the way white images on black background do. It is more difficult to penetrate because on a computer black resembles a block without perception of depth. Thus, if a thief penetrates the zone, the computer would lock onto the dark image and that individual would find themselves penned in by quickly descending metal doors. Or if your thief becomes isolated in a room, the doors and windows lock. Generally your protective device, be it a dark image of trees or a skyline, is coded as a generic scheme making penetration of your electronic system virtually impossible."

"I see. Was the system made up of pictures that were ever exhibited?"

"Later as Mr. Roark felt a more sophisticated system was needed. That's why our consultant felt it was an inside job."

"Did Genieve's name ever come up?"

"No."

"What about Knowles Hauptman?"

"Yes, but not with regard to harassment. Hauptman died, they think, as a result of a fall."

"How old was he when he died?"

"Twenty-two. He was a young kid."

"How did the father take the news?"

"He was in New York at the time. He didn't hear of it until several hours later and he was understandably overcome with grief. In fact my direct supervisor paid for a police retiree to be available for him."

"That was considerate. Did his son work for him?"

"No. Knowles was the followup act to a bartender who worked at his mother's lounge in Sausalito. It was where he met his wife."

"Probably where he got his divorce."

"Probably," Ames remarked, chortling. "In any event the problem with the stolen art was they produced imposters after the son's death."

"Do you have any thoughts about that?"

"I think the imposters were meant to wear this guy Hauptman down by looking similar enough to the art on his security monitors. It probably took him awhile to realize his art was stolen. Then his son was killed. Then someone flooded the market with copies of his security controls."

"Did you ever come up with a name?"

"As to who went to all the trouble? No. By the time we latched onto the group we thought was setting the stage, they left town to the Midwest and a new group was operating. We eventually turned over our file to the FBI."

"Can you give me the name of your contact there?"

"Special Agent in Command Thomas Garvey."

"Out of San Rafael?"

"I don't know where he's based. That's the man's name."

The world of Special Agent in Command Garvey extended as far as farm contracts with the state were granted. I knew the Australian agent with wingtip shoes, a Movado wristwatch and wide brim hat as the man the state looked to for problems with security breaks of institutions — medical labs, sperm banks, morgues, computer virus galleries. For the five or six occasions I had been selected to provide information to the agent's team, I knew Garvey to have a steel-trap mind and dogged perseverance that won him cases long after the evidence was cold.

"FBI." Thomas Garvey answered, after the first ring.

"Lennis Cliford."

"Good to hear from you, Investigator. What can I do for you?"

"I'm researching a possible blackmail scheme for an influential socialite. I just finished talking with Officer Ames."

"Computer crime is his specialty."

"He's got some good ideas. Does the name Neil Holyer mean anything to you?"

"We've broken down that case into a half dozen files, none which offer much beside computer snags. Most police jurisdictions see this sort of work all over the state."

"What's your interest?"

"The protections go with deeds, most which were amended in Superior Courts in those counties where the computer intrusions occurred. As to the date box he brought in, we've been keeping tabs on that thing for a year with some interesting returns."

"Can you tell me?"

"At this point it's no longer classified. Most of these computer crimes involving semi-large corporations have utilized changes in designation of land use. As the state permits sloughs to dry up and water to be redirected, farmland previously utilized only for crops change and the changes become public record."

"Are you saying that the systems break-ins you are investigating involve state controlled systems?"

"Yes," Special Agent in Command Garvey replied, adding, "we have discovered we can more easily track thefts if their information is derived by recent map changes. The problem for Holyer is that while the map is not the territory, the map is nevertheless conveyed by an actual boundary and anyone smart enough to take snapshots of the actual land boundary can conceivably bust into the system."

"Who do you suspect has hacked into the systems of Holyer's social circle?"

"Because of his wealth, we think it's someone close to him who would know what the impact on his system would be."

"Such as his son?"

"The consultant to Ames, man by the last name of Frear, thought it was a member of his security firm."

I nodded into the phone. "Any idea what they were after?"

"We think their objective may have been hard money such as the Berlin diamond or installed art."

"Why the diamond?"

"Roark displays a priceless diamond on the top floor and the security is set up similar to that of the Lourve with the apex ceiling, red lights like a runway at night, mirrors at angles in the entry and mirrors at the rear of the display room with cameras."

"Is the stone worth much?"

"It is valued roughly at ninety million. The thing with Roark's social circle is these seven or eight individuals serve on a board of directors for the museum."

"Any possibility this is organized crime?"

"It's organized, we just don't know yet by whom."

I picked up my son at Amtrak at Jack London Square. Marion was down for a day before he went by train to see his father in Bakersfield.

We went to Spenger's Fish Grotto for dinner. He ordered abalone and I had mahi mahi and a vodka and tonic. He had met a young woman who was majoring in fates and sirens and composing her own Ballo del Granduca. She had written the poems and music for the operetta, chosen an impresario, and written the grand finale.

"She sounds very talented."

Marion smiled at me through languid blue eyes that would always remind me of his father. "She gets to direct all the stage sets too."

"That's a huge project, Sweetheart."

"No kidding. A real capo aria."

"So tell me again: what's the plot?"

"It takes place in Venice because the city was richer than Rome. The gods emerge from the sea and sit in heaven, their ship turns into a rock, Ulysses is hit by a sword of fire and the Trojan Wars begin. There's an alto tenor who sings about a naval battle at sea and transvestites who sing about the bloodshed, magic and missing people."

"Well, that sounds like fun. Will you let me know when it is?"

We went through our usual list. He answered my questions dutifully, a polite son, who would soon enter tournaments and competitions and he'd enter the age of manhood where scorn of one's upbringing would outdistance his need to come see me every quarter, and I'd become forgotten. After dinner we took our customary drive to revisit the places of my childhood, a requisite passion for him despite the intolerances he was picking up.

I drove across town to the Gilman exit and headed into north Berkeley up Marin to the circle with a green concrete fountain of gargoyles. Marion and I chatted about the nature of uncertainties, he doing most of the talking. He said some small undefined thing out of his youth begged to be noticed. It was not about security, for in those days he had no need for such protections, nor was it about memories and missed opportunities, but he felt something seemed to hint at wrong paths chosen if only because what was wanted was not what had materialized.

I talked to him as I drove up Los Angeles Avenue past the house of an elementary school chum of mine whose father worked for Home Office, his brick home the city of Berkeley's concept of Daphne Du Maurier's Frenchman's Creek, next door to which a child in 1956 lost his life when he was playing in a vacant lot and was shut inside a block of opaque glass the size of a refrigerator — one of the last few houses built entirely of four-inch wood walls remaining in Berkeley, its value largely increased by the fact that the homes that burned in the Berkeley/Oakland firestorm had all been replaced by second and third story stone mansions, all slab foundations, all with a minimum of wood including the roofs. I was seized by a parent's absolute knowledge that Marion's feeling was all important, that he was saying goodbye to some aspect of himself and I didn't want to miss out. We would have this moment for the rest of our lives and could refer to it with relief and humor.

At the corner of Los Angeles and Spruce sat my best friend's house, a superb rendition of a corner brown shingle, within healthy walking distance to stores and coffee houses situated on Vine and Shattuck and Chez Panisse and the former Co-op market, which had the first and only daycare center for the children of shoppers. While most of the houses along Spruce Street were exterior stucco to begin with, deemed a good way to keep the home at a cool 76 degrees during 85 degree summers well into an Indian summer in late October, their all wood counterparts, smaller than seven hundred square feet, on Shattuck and Oxford bordering Live Oaks park where in the '70s the San Francisco Mime Troupe would give free plays, were enhanced by creekbeds and deeply rooted Oak trees wedged up to the foundations, brick patios, fountains, climbing ivy and decks. I crossed Marin at an angle to Santa Barbara past the Indian rocks, all a sandstone jumble of boulders, up some three city blocks from the actual Indian Rock park. Marion said, pointing out the window, isn't that the famed Burdick home, who put crystal windows off a private study inside which Eugene Burdick, playwright and novelist, wrote The Ugly American, a carpeted beauty of solid wood exterior and the best teak floors money could buy. An alley directly across led to an unused garage made of brick and on one side to the engineering professor at UC Berkeley and to the other, a brick two story home with a wooden balcony and wooden stairs leading to a lawn, slate patio and bed of roses, my home. On Santa Barbara beside us, down a rolling green, the Chinese man whose presence was known only by the paper lanterns he lit at night during summer months. The author Nabosek, his novel Lolita more shocking than most lifestyles of the day would ever conjure up, lived on San Luis perched above a staircase of stones laid into the soil, also one of the few solidly wood houses inside and out. Further down the street the house fronting one of the first stone staircases was built in the fashion of the Norwegian, made of wood but with a predominantly tile interior, its morning room which looked out over John Hinckle Park and the theatre house. For the rose garden at San Luis and Southhampton, to the iron gates fronting a small woman's college, its tiled pool with concrete heads of lesser gods, to the Arlington sat the last stand of wood dream homes with small strips of windows on northern walls, sunlight oblique and fading no matter the time of day, tucked in between stucco and stone tall, thin houses whose interiors contained a spacious kitchen with breakfast nook, wood paneled den, wood floors in the dining and living rooms and three bedrooms on the top floors beneath massive attics with dormers.

"We've got to get back. I don't want to miss my train," he said, and I went out the Arlington and headed to the train station.

CHAPTER 4.

I WOULD BE A DETECTIVE FOR LIFE, long after my son had grown comfortably into his midlife. There I'd be, older, possibly stymied or not, content or not, bills and mortgage paid off, my questions answered and perhaps long forgotten. I would remember snapshots, all-wood houses in south Berkeley between Gilman and University with Victorian fronts were sold by the city to indigents for a dollar each. Interested buyers were told not another home in Berkeley would ever be built entirely of wood walls again. This, because the value for homes became marked by two things only — the square footage and the presence of soft wood flooring, mahogany considered ideal for walls and ash better for mounted ceilings with copper, jade or plank for doors; sandstone for siding.

"The system Wes finally opted for was based upon photographs of light. Panels of light in quick succession intermixed by a collection of lithographs of art. On a satellite system this produced flashes of light said to identify diamonds in transport so they could not be stolen," said Schuyler Frear, the consultant on artists works situated at the Oakland Police Department. Thin, medium height, balding, wire rim eye glasses, he advised Bay Area jurisdictions from Monterey to Sacramento and was called upon daily to provide expertise of one type or another.

We sat in his small office, the thin window in the room muting the sunlight along with errant reflective light from the traffic on the street. His desk was stacked with files and his metal filing cabinets bulged with papers, making the office seem over utilized despite all accommodations of technology — a computer with high speed Internet access, several printers, cameras with digital diskettes, a television monitor and a window into a small interview booth outfitted with consoles.

"The collection of lithographs were actually representations of farmland in various cities predominantly in the western United States. The Hauptman collection was mostly watercolor abstracts of marsh areas and farm plots of southern Louisiana, for example, Mt. Rainier flatlands, the Idaho lowlands, Oregon interior, California delta, Salinas valley, and so on. Oddly enough, numerous attempts have been made to steal these."

"Why would someone steal them?"

"Any number of practical reasons." He reached for a book of building illustrations over which were pencilled shadings and gradations of segments which overlay areas of each panel. "The watercolors are used as maps to doctor each illustration."

"Yes, I can see how that would work."

"It's popular appeal that holds the Hauptman collection in high regard because the military uses similar patterning to track missing objects."

I could appreciate the implications. Roark owned a museum, his son had cracked security codes, there were any number of viable art fences at the ready to abscond with valuables which once stolen would drive up the net worth of the items.

"It gets quite complicated," Schuyler said. "Security firms house their archives with various other database vaults for protection. When a piece is stolen, these vaults are referenced and if as has occurred on occasion files have been tampered, you know you have a security leak."

"You must track each item meticulously."

"Absolutely. With the last harassment prank to Mr. Holyer's garden, it is rather disconcerting to find the changes made on the files corresponded in kind to items in text of these same lithographs."

"I didn't realize that to be the case. What do you believe the thief wanted?"

"That remains to be seen. Our thought was that Roark or someone in his line had connections to diamond manufacturers whose aims were to dismember his security systems in order to successfully take his diamond. That could explain the degree of harassment he and his friends have over the years been subjected to."

"Were you aware Teresa D'Coteur Roark responded to a ransom demand?"

"No. When would this have been?"

"A week ago. The note asked for money from two accounts — hers and her son's. She did not keep the note."

Schuyler had removed a yellow legal pad and was taking down the information in a rapid scrawl. "Why the son's?"

"Not known. She thinks it was because Roark himself was inaccessible. The note asked for a hundred thousand."

"Did she retain you?"

"Yes. I queried Roark who informed me that a young woman claiming to be the son's wife showed up with a child bearing an uncanny resemblance to the son, and asked for money. He wrote her a check for two thousand."

"Damn, why the hell don't these people put in an official call? Does Ms. D'Coteur have any idea of the art theft from Mr. Holyer?"

"She didn't mention it to me."

"Well ask, will you, when you talk to her next? Half her social circle has been hit."

"I heard."

"Yes, the entire thing reeks of a ring."

"I thought the same thing. In fact, I went to talk to Randall who told me he's making out alright on two jobs — one pumping gas and the other clerking for a small grocery counter. Obstinate as hell. He inferred this young woman would show the moment I left."

"Typical. You planning on setting up listening posts or wire taps?"

"Nothing until something definite materializes. I ran a criminal history on the female — she's got a hit for writing bad checks and for forgery."

"We'll keep an eye out. Good luck. Any leads?"
I had one. It was for Mitchel Hauptman.

It was not yet noon and the day was warming up to be a scorcher. A canopy of green leaves hung above the street like a fur wrap. The highway divided at the Richmond turnoff and I wended my way around the bend onto 880 West toward the Richmond Bridge and Tamalpais landmark. The freeway enlarged from a single lane in each direction to four lanes at Marina. Boat repair shops lined up, some inside yards with high guard surveillance, others in simple wire fences, mostly sailboats with blue awning cloth on the mast.

At one time I drove a two door, white Ford coupe with red leather seats. My first trip in it was to Terra Linda. I rode with an associate who was six months short of her needed private investigator license. We rode a ferry from Point Molate to an island and aviary and that night ate at the Dock in Tiburon. It was a relaxing day and I at twenty-one found myself thinking I was going to live forever, agile and self assured.

Randall was a different sort, a young man with possibilities for whom failure would not spell impending doom. In time he might steer portage to the island aviary or get a job as a janitor at any of dozens of Julia Morgan or Frank Lloyd Wright halls or cottages. None of it would hurt if by age forty he was finally disgusted with dabbling and decided to apply himself to a career as a programmer or consultant.

Mitchel Hauptman's home was a two story made mostly of glass and steel beams tucked into an ivy laden slope overlooking the Sausalito harbor. His home occupied a terrace and possessed a thick ebony door with opaque glass panels, a slate patio, and an abrupt wall with maidenfern, misted and forlorn, dangling over a waterfall and fishpond. The front room opened onto a narrow window which at once took in Angel Island and the street and pier where The Soundless Wave restaurant perched, a low surround of tinted glass with a bluish wooden walkway and gravel lot.

Hauptman was five foot nine, medium build, good physique, somewhat broodish, brown hair, suntanned, plaid red, green and white collared shirt, knit trousers and salmon socks.

"I've come about Wesley Roark's son," I said to the man who by his telling expression indicated he knew about the situation.

"Mitchel Hauptman," he said gruffly.

We shook hands. Mitchel led me down two stairs into a den off the living room. From here one glimpsed elegant houseboats docked at the Waldo Point gated community.

"Schuyler called," Mitchel explained. "I gather Roark's son has put everyone through their paces again."

I removed my notepad and pen. "Has he done this before?"

"Several times. He worked for me one summer you know."

"I thought it was two."

"No, just one. I had a small office and gallery in the city at the time. He's a smart lad."

"What did he do?"

"The usual. Sent out payments on bills, ordered supplies, stocked the place."

"What year would this have been?"

"2000."

"Did he handle anything out of the ordinary? Accounts?"

"No, no," Hauptman pooh poohed the idea. "I've two accountants for my sales."

"And you didn't interest him in security?"

"Wouldn't dream of it."

"Did he ever come here?"

"Few times. I gave him a key for weekends."

"And he had run of the place?"

Mitchel nodded, smiling. "He was like a little puppy dog."

"His mother is fearful he's trying to blackmail her. She received a demand that asked her to dump out her son's account."

"I'd be surprised if it's Randall. He'd have no use for a large amount of money."

"Apparently he has a son with a young woman."

"Randall?"

"Yes. Did you give him access to your studio?"

"It's locked. The screens are there; but the computers are on the second floor where my equipment is."

"Does anyone else live with you?"

"My wife. Her name is Jess. If you're still here in a half hour you can meet her. She's out running errands."

"Does she know Randall?"

"I'd be surprised if she's spoken as much as a sentence to him in the past year."

"Do you or your wife talk to Mr. Roark or either of his wives?"

"We have occasional contact with Genieve. We didn't know Terry to speak of, and then we have mutual friends. Neil Holyer — "

"The art collector?"

"Yes. He shops for me."

"Does he have any of your posters?"

"One. Mine are quite pricey. Each one is upward of thirty thousand."

"They represent security abstractions."

"Yes, but if you're suggesting young Randall took one in order to gain some sort of entrance to his father's system for example — "

"I am."

"No, it wouldn't work that way. The prints are merely snapshots of a single frame and are not in fact copies of the motion sequence which at any time secures the establishment it is designed for."

"Any possibility Randall designed his own set of patterns and replaced any part of the sequences?"

Mitchel gave me a sobering gaze. His mouth pulled tightly over a narrow sunken cheekbone structure and tugged at his square jaw. "Anything is possible. People do it all the time. That's the drawback for on-line systems. But he would have to design a system that is made up of abstract images. In addition he would have to be very astute with maneuvering camera shots. Not that it couldn't be done. It'd take a hell of a lot of skill though."

"I believe the police think he has the skill. Do you know what his parents own that he might desire to acquire?"

"His father has the museum; he has a private exhibition hall in his bank with expensive art, not to mention a world famous diamond, and he oversees buying and trading on the international marketplace. That should keep any young person sufficiently amused."

"How about paintings, stamps, original Hollywood costumes?"

"Yes," he replied. "I see what you mean. Items that are easily fenced. Randall doesn't need to wire cut through an alarm system for those. He can walk into any number of summer homes and fence the art. The things he'd be trying to get his hands on with the security would be tapes — of people entering, leaving, storing items, setting clocks, sending by post, hallways, archives, windows, the parking lot and so on."

"Who would most likely be interested in purchasing this sort of thing?"

"Anyone, that's the trouble." Something caused him to glance up and he rose saying, "Ah, Jess, my dear, please meet Investigator Cliford."

Jess Hauptman was a friendly looking, petite blonde with short wavy hair. She stood about five feet and wore a powder blue cotton dress with a white jacket and matching pumps and gloves. "Pleased to meet you, Ms. Cliford." Her voice like her manner was soft, pleasant. "How can we help you?"

We sat comfortably, Jess ready to be of assistance. "Ms. Cliford wants to know whether you permitted young Roark here when you were here?"

"Only once. When Knowles was still living. Randall must have been what," pausing to look inquiringly at her husband, "not yet fifteen. He wanted a peek at the studio so I showed it to him. He actually wanted a look at the database but Mitchel wasn't home and I don't touch my husband's study without his permission."

"You think it was mere curiosity?"

"I couldn't say. He said his father had a poster inside his study and that he had taken a color photograph of it which he wanted to put on the computer. Something like that."

"Really?" Her husband asked, surprised. "I didn't know."

"Yes," she said, a look of fondness at him, "and he wanted to experiment with color."

Mitchel chuckled. "It's my machine that produces the design based upon desired angle and depth of light."

"I found it odd too," she said.

I gave a nod. "Could he damage his father's security, say for the bank vault?"

Mitchel answered. "Not likely. But the museum would be another matter. The system used to have no replacement when its stations failed."

"You ought to speak to Genieve," Jess said. "It's possible she sees through her stepson's actions better than the rest of us."

"Good idea," Mitchel said. "I believe she took over management of the museum after Teresa left. She might know what set of circumstances thrust Randall out the door."

They walked me to the door. Jess said, half jokingly, "I always thought of Randall as Genieve's son. Once Teresa left, and Wes remarried, Randall sort of let loose. He had full run of that home — "

"It was substantial," Mitchel remarked in agreement.

"And he seemed more at ease, although I guess he had too

much freedom."

"Did he know your son well?"

"Yes. He worked with him in San Rafael at the warehouse."

"Did you find your son?"

"No, we were in New York. Genieve did."

"Was she your son's wife?"

"Yes," Mitchel said. "They were going through a divorce when he died."

"Did Genieve offer any explanation as to what happened?"

"Just that he fell. He was drunk."

"Was he drunk often?"

"Daily." He was evasive as though this somehow reflected poorly on him. "We suspected she was seeing another man. Even so," he said, to be generous, "she was pretty wrecked over it."

"Where were they residing when your son died?"

"Inverness. Her sister-in-law resides there now. That's Sally Ann Roark, although she's recently divorced. Fourth marriage."

"Can you give me the address?"

"It's easy enough to find. It sits at the end of the road before the state park beach. It's a one story Eichler." He rattled off an address. Then: "Genieve still owns the restaurant you see below the house here."

"The Soundless Wave?"

"That's the one."

Sail boats glided over the peaceful water. Beyond them the Angel Island Ferry crossed the bay to the island where hundred year wooden piers once used for Chinese camps still remained intact. For those who could afford it, life was a state of leisure, blissful, unencumbered.

I walked to the restaurant entrance. A jazz rendition of Beethoven's Ninth bleated through the speaker system. Once inside, my eyes adjusted to the dim light. Photographs of predominantly African American movie stars and rock concert impresarios covered a wall. Lionel Ritchie stood in his normal casual attire of long shirt, white denims and tennis shoes chatting amicably with the female lead for the musical couple Ashford and Simpson. Also on the wall were the singer I had spoken to at Terry's party and her piano player.

I stepped up to the bar. "Nice place you've got here," I said to the bartender, a New York looking bloke dressed for the A's game on the overhead television.

"Thanks, mate," the bartender barked back. "What's it going to be?"

"Cup of expresso."

"Will do. You a cop?"

"Investigator, from Oakland area."

"What brings you down this way?"

"Work. Do you know Carole Price?"

"I do indeed." The man grinned. "I used to date her. She and the owner were pretty tight at one time. By the way, the name's Ted Jones." He rambled on as he steamed the coffee. "Carole was a real beauty in her day. Her family had a home over there in Berkeley near Clark Kerr campus, a glass walled in house at the corner. Gen — she was Genieve Canber in those days — lived at the Price home until she met and married the physician Knowles Hauptman, whose family was residing out of Louisiana."

"Was it a good marriage?"

"I would've thought so, but you never know. Many of us thought he was killed by organized crime."

"Any particular reason?"

"Well, this is strictly rumor, but he had a string of warehouses in San Rafael where he housed glass, new art deco type stuff, and there were a series of mishaps there that left him broke as a whistle. After he began the emergency rooms at Bay Area hospitals, he kissed that life goodbye."

"Did you think the mishaps followed him?"

"Some sort of trouble followed him because he's dead. If not for that, he'd be part owner today, don't you think?"

I didn't know what to think. "Do you manage the place for Mrs. Roark?"

"No, I'm part owner. Genieve comes in once a month, if that, and eyeballs the books. I plan the meals with the chef, order in the bar, keep the work schedule and so on. Our silent partner is Mitchel Hauptman who keeps the cash flowing if there's a problem."

"I heard her first husband died on a holiday weekend."

"True enough. It was July Fourth weekend and we were scheduled to bring in a dixie band who called that week to say their bus had broken down in Alabama and they couldn't make the date. Carole actually did all the sets that holiday."

"Good thing she had the availability."

"It is," he replied, and served the expresso with a dash of cinnamon and a sprig of freeze-dried lemon. "She had been singing at the Fairmont on and off and at the Claremont Hotel for summer revues. As it turned out she had that summer off."

"What caused Hauptman's plunge to be fatal? Was he as drunk as his mother let on?"

"Oh, you talked to her?"

"Just came from there."

"They're a nice couple." Setting down his glass, he said, "Knowles was an independent spirit. Everything he did he did on the sauce. He tried his hand at writing for Hollywood. Then he spent six, seven years in film school making film shorts, but it got too expensive. So he went to College of New York and studied art intending to become an artist like Geneva's father, Jaime Canber. Knowles did a few shows, nothing that amounted to much. Finally in the eleventh hour he came to work here for me.

"If the police say his post mortem said he was drunk, then he was pie-faced. It wouldn't have been unusual."

"Ever have to drive him home?"

"Stuck him in a cab was more like it. At least three to four times a week."

"Was it just addiction?"

"Knowles was a spoiler. He was too undefined, too chatty. He had no sense of emotional preservation."

"But then you see that often with longtime alcoholics."

"No kidding. Can I fix you another?"

"No, thanks. How did Genieve take his death?"

"It wrecked her. She was pretty spent, slept alot."

"Prescribed tranks?"

"A handful. Her physician, friend of the other guy, dropped in on her weekly to monitor her. I guess she was doing about as well as could be expected."

"Was Genieve married before she met Hauptman?"

"Genieve married a songwriter when she was in her late teens." He waited as I took a sip of coffee and nodded appreciatively.

"Excellent." I said.

"Glad you like it. They had a child who lives in Menlo Park. The guy had a fatal accident over a July weekend oddly enough. After Knowles' death she was known pejoratively by his friends as a Black Widow." He poured himself a Seven-up and shrugged, saying, "People can be cruel. You know how it is."

"What about her sister-in-law on the Roark side?"

"Sally Ann?"

"Think she'll talk to me?"

"I don't see why not. It's not as if she's a recluse."

"Thanks for your time," I said, and slapped a five on the counter. "Great place," I said, taking in the walls of continuous windows and plush emerald carpet.

CHAPTER 5.

THE DRIVE TO INVERNESS took me up the coast some twenty miles. The afternoon was sedate and the air balmy with a hint of swollen expectation as if the sky might produce rain. Rusted propane pumps languished on dilapidated harbors and sailboats tied to buoys crested on waves as each motorboat churned full throttle through the waterway. I passed a market that advertised beer, newspapers, fresh vegetables and pharmacy. Approximately six miles up the road at the approach to the state park stood the alleged home.

It was obvious Eichler, the wood long faded and tarnished by rains and sun and wind. Windows appeared at forty-five degree angles at the roof level and at the door.

"Ted called to tell me you were coming," Sally Ann Roark said, as she led me through an outdoor patio to a living room that overlooked a half acre lot of tan oak trees.

We sat at a dining room table next to a burning log in the hearth. The floor space appeared modest, maybe nine hundred square feet. A kitchen and a bath and bedroom all overlooked the same tag of forest.

She was an average looking blonde, not charismatic as Genieve was. Medium height, silvery blonde, soft. Her blue eyes were also soft.

"This is an older home." I remarked.

"Yes, I purchased it from my sister-in-law."

"It's beautiful. Comfortable."

"Thank you. Can I fix tea?"

"No, I'm fine. I was hoping you could tell me how your brother-in-law died."

Her eyes were soft and beautiful, full of understated meaning. "I honestly don't know. Genieve, I'm told, was sleeping and woke out of sleep. Knowles wasn't in bed, so she slipped on a robe and went looking for him. The garden lights were on which was strange. She walked out onto the patio and that's when she saw him in the pool."

"I didn't realize he drowned. Did she attempt to rescue him?"

"She did, but his body was like a weight. I believe she tried to clear his airway but couldn't revive him. The sheriff-coroner said there was nothing that could've been done. Apparently Knowles was drunk at the time of death."

"How long was she married to him?"

"They tied the knot in 1982."

"So they were married for how many years?"

"Eleven years, and before that she was married to her first husband for five years."

"She married him in — ?"

"In 1970, after dating him for five years."

"These were no fly-by-night romances."

"No, they weren't."

"What about her recent marriage to Mr. Roark?"

"Wes?" At my prompting, she answered, "She met my brother in 1988."

I turned to a blank page in my notepad. "I understand she and your brother have been continually harassed."

"We all were for a time. I was followed to and from my office so frequently I closed it and operated from my home. With Wes it was worse. They badgered him at his office in the city and at home."

"Over what?"

"His bank apparently."

"But you don't know why?"

"No, no idea."

"Could the harassment you spoke of have come about as a result of your brother's investments?"

"They could." Her tone said she was a realist who after years of bitter scrutiny settled for any explanation she could readily part with in favor of the truth, if she could decide what that consisted of.

"How did Genieve take Hauptman's death?"

"Badly. She threw herself into refurbishing the restaurant with expensive designer pieces which consumed her time and energies."

"Did her friend Holyer help with purchases?"

"I don't think so. These were pieces made by Warren McArthur, Donald Deskey, Paul Frankel and such — not the sort of thing Neil goes for. They're known for wood and aluminum furniture for modern studios. They were the first contemporaries."

"You're quite knowledgeable."

"My first husband bought these lines. After our divorce I studied these people. It's how I met Mitchel and Knowles. Are you familiar with Kem Weber? I spent five years around Fort Mason and alternately in Brisbane and Millbrae and the modern designers were sought after, even in the architectural styles." She was at ease, in control of the content of what would pass for dialogue between them. "We were all fans of those period pieces, especially of Bel Geddes, Michael Breuer and Gilbert Rohde, who was very metal, glass and Formica oriented."

I was out of my element and I guessed my blank look exposed me.

She explained. "Design in America owes a great deal to these innovators. The modernists, as they were called. They weren't Art Deco. Their lines were more consistent with geometric, industrial-produced styles for a mass market. I think Mitchel was skeptical of Geneva's intentions. She was convinced steel and glass were the next horizon; and was investing a fair amount of their stocks. Not only that, Geneva's father was a well-known artist and his work brought in a good sum. His family had original title to the tan oak forests from Berkeley to Hayward and San Ramon."

"Who in the family had title?"

"Her great grandfather, Jedediah Canber."

"Did your father see that money?"

"No. By 1931 it was in dispute. The university was said to own it, but my brother kept documents that show the university was not given that land until 1959. I have the deed. Here, I'll get it."

She left the living room. I walked to the wall sized window and gazed at the gnarled oak trees, their ashen bark marred by light green lichen. For a woman in her late fifties with artistic perceptions of the world, Sally Ann had a privacy few could afford. The coin-shaped brown leaves that lay over the soil formed an intriguing carpet to the forty or more trees that shaded the acre lot.

When she returned with a framed document, she loosened the metal tabs and handed me the delicate brochure. I put on my eyeglasses, carefully opened it and examined it. It was a deed for a fifty thousand acre parcel land including trees, but it was written as a deed to a village. It was notarized by Bank of Jamaica and dated June 22, 1897.

"May I copy the information?"

"I'll make you a copy. I have a Xerox machine."

It struck me that the enormity of her family's previous land holdings should have been able to oversee almost any venture the heirs would later decide upon. When she returned, I asked, "What was the dispute over exactly?"

"Her grandfather was said to have committed a crime for which the judgement against him was forty thousand acres. Her father fought the sentence, and lost."

"In what court did this occur?"

"Oakland, in 1950. My brother was enormously intrigued by this history, partly because our family going back to that year attempted to acquire part of that ranch."

"And Knowles? Did he know about this land debate?"

"Yes. We all did. In fact while he was married to Genieve, she sold a portion in 1979 to the state."

"What did she do with the money?"

"She purchased the restaurant outright along with a two hundred thousand dollar houseboat at Waldo Point and paid off what was outstanding on this home."

"It doesn't go far these days."

"No." She laughed.

"Did you ever meet the first Mrs. Wesley Roark?"

"Of course. I know both wives."

"What about her son Randall?"

"I met him a handful of times at the Hauptmans."

"I was told Mitchel hired Randall one summer to handle inventory for his studio in the city."

"I met him at various computer multimedia shows. Randall's interest in light was shared by the Hauptmans."

"What was Randall's interest?"

"How to produce filtered light within a building's interior."

"Any possibility Knowles Hauptman lost his life to the same investments?"

"Anything is possible, Ms. Cliford. We all learn too late that the things we most admire in other people's lives are those activities we could live without. It was everyone's opinion that Knowles lost his life in the most beautiful garden only a gardener could do justice to. Both he and my brother loved the same woman and more or less had the same ambitions."

The past had its template and doors to it were closed. I hoped those doors stayed closed for Randall Roark but feared if anyone could open them it would be a teen with a passion for breaking into sophisticated databases.

"Do you know what Knowles was investing in when he died?"

"Electronic surveillance for residences."

I thanked her. All tracks looped in reverse to the thing that preceded it — like a confession.

CHAPTER 6.

THE BAY GLITTERED. Where there had been mud flats at 2:53pm on the previous day, at high tide the water covered the banks and splashed against a jetty of rocks. At the edge of the Richmond oil wells sat the castle, an empty warehouse that might have contained rusting cans of oil sludge or transmission refuse but for some reason had become over the years closed off from human access. The small sailboat that I had seen beached and precariously tipped to its starboard side, now bobbed peacefully on the water. Birds like salt and pepper floated on the milky white water. A piece of driftwood, half submerged, caught my eye.

The condominiums stood like tall loan sharks at the edge of the forest of Eucalyptus on the western side of Albany Hill. The sun rose and set over shades drawn to protect the elderly or nearly sightless. Mora Silver's sixth floor apartment captured an exquisite span of water and the distant hump of the peninsula on which Sausalito was nestled. In the foreground yachts glided effortlessly, a catamaran or two in the bunch. Further off, Mount Tamalpais rose into the cloudless sky.

Eyes of long dead actresses peered from oval frames beneath golden brass light fixtures. Prisms in the chandelier broke the afternoon sunlight into a rainbow shawl which lay over a pink and green damask sofa.

Her hair was her outstanding feature. It was blondish white with a silver sheen. Gentle waves coiffed her demure face. She was slender, medium height, and her arms were waxen white against a velvet burgundy sleeveless blouse. Pale blue eyes gave her the striking resemblance to her niece.

"Yes, I married Gunther more on a lark. He'd just opened a computer firm and was bringing in state-of-the-art electronics. He was a handsome man in those days."

"Did Randall spend much time with him?"

"Randall? He was a toddler, maybe two or three. His father doted on him. Terry on the other hand was ambitious and rarely at home. Usually she had him packed off to Vera's, a friend of Teresa's."

"What about to — what's his name? Ted?"

She smiled, her face lighting up with fond remembrance. "Teddy. He was my sweetheart in the old days before any of them tied the knot and married."

She spoke as if she were actually much older than she was. He hadn't impressed me as older than sixty-five and Terry was not yet sixty. "Did he ever marry?"

"To a singer whose name was Georgia. She was a singer then, an amazingly resonant voice. She had a lot of life in her then. She was at those box car races like clockwork along with Bobby Gamble."

"Gamble? He's a big name in the box car events, isn't he?"

"Gamble drove for Bud Light and Tide for several years, taking the Cup one year at San Bernardino's Orange Bowl. The crowds loved him."

"How old is Gamble today?"

"Seventy-four. Carole's age."

"Does he live out here on the West coast?"

"In Albany actually. He retired. Teresa can tell you, or Vera if she has an address to be found. He survived one race and took a tumble in another a year later, then brushed fate with a wall. It was time. He had to get out."

"So you were altogether in the same social circle?"

"Yes. There were Teresa and Wes, Carole and Teddy, Vera and Gamble, myself and Gunther, Wesley's friends the Hauptmans with their son and my niece who was his wife Geneva. And a handful of other couples and singles who came and went over the years."

"Neil Holyer?"

"Holyer, right. The antique dealer. About fifty people in

all. We led a privileged life. Art shows, museum exhibits, car races, thrills — we burned the candle at both ends. As he got older Randall fit right in."

"In what way?"

"Wes got him his first automobile when he turned twelve, a Corvette, orange exterior, aqua green trim, aqua green interior, all silver chrome, wooden dash, whitewalls, a gorgeous chunk of change."

"Does Randall still have it?"

"He traded it in for a Duesenberg. This was orange with white bucket seats. Gamble trained him to ride it, until the car was sold two years later."

"It sounds as though Randall was exposed to the jet set."

"The poor man's version of the rich. Nothing you or I'll ever see."

"Your place here is not exactly modest," I said, referring to a spacious living room adjoining an elegant dining room with bookshelves and expensive antique furniture, what looked to be a spacious kitchen with sunroof, another sitting room beyond it and through a door what might be a bedroom.

She shrugged. "I'm lucky to have this suite, certainly. It's twenty-two hundred square feet, but it's not the Ritz. Of all of us, myself and Carole lost the most to camera-shot poses."

"I beg your pardon?"

"It's what I call the vagaries of misfortune. When I was still married to Gunther we had an opportunity to purchase a flat on Bourbon Street in New Orleans, but I felt I wouldn't care to reside there without being close to my friends. Carole had gone her own way by then, drifting into the artist and jazz dungeons of San Pablo with her man friend Magnes, and Neil was turning over a new leaf by getting out of the computer industry and focussing on cardboard acquisitions and then the Hauptmans lost their son."

"Was that in the same year?"

"More or less, maybe six months apart. It didn't stop there.

The losses piled up that year. Following his death I lost my sister, Geneva's mother. Trust me, if anyone's death was going to do someone in, it was Laurdres. Laurdres never knew what she had, right up to the day of her death. She threw it all away — looks, husband, everything — when she wrapped that ZX of theirs around a tree." Her bitterness was a heavier chip than the small change of blown glass that adorned the fireplace mantel and glass case. "She was a terrible flirt, a worse drinker. It wasn't just the men she flirted with but danger, recklessness, bungee jumping, racing, you name it."

I gazed about at the oddities of chartreuse, opaque and green sculpture twisted into unrelenting shapes. Her rant was of a once-dutiful wife who since she lost the comfort of marriage had also lost some undefinable aspect of appreciation to a sister who sucked dry whatever remained of goodwill.

"What was Laurdres like as a parent?" I asked.

"Very self willed. Whatever she wanted, Geneva was expected to comply with. She refused to let Geneva cry. Trust me, children cry. They have upsets or disappointments and they cry. But my sister had this idea that some agency in San Francisco would make her child a model for commercials on television. Laurdres wouldn't allow as much as a whimper. She dominated her, oversaw every nuance."

"Did Geneva like her mother?"

"Yes, she doted on her, admired her style of dress, manner, lifestyle."

"Does she resemble her mother?"

"To a degree. You have to remember Laurdres was vivacious whereas Gen is cultivated, cool. Laur was fiery, undisciplined, unwilling to follow anyone else's lead; Gen is reserved, careful. Too careful in my opinion."

"But not distancing in the way her mother was to her," I said, in an attempt to ferret out the relationship between the second Mrs. Roark and the stepson.

"Well, she's not exactly solicitous of her stepson. He moved out because of her. I think it's why he feels he's not welcome there, why when he does go home it's to his mother's home."

"Were you aware he had withdrawn a hundred thousand?"

"How on earth would he do that?"

"That's what I am looking into. It seems he may have participated in a ransom demand."

She considered this. "It doesn't seem likely he would do that because he can have access to his father's account at any time simply by asking. Do you know what he did with the money?"

"He has a wife and year-old baby."

"Randall? He's seventeen."

"I know, but some teens figure out their life earlier than the rest of us. He has a cabin in Canyon. It's not much of an existence but it seems to be what he wants."

"But he has the rest of his life ahead of him." Her voice had the hint of rising alarm. "Why would he throw it away?"

"Her name is Jane Hart. Ever met her?"

"No, never heard of her."

"Apparently Ms. Hart presented herself and the baby to Mr. Roark and he wrote her a check."

"He's gone the path of Carole Price."

"The singer? Flamboyant redhead?"

"That's her."

"She and Ted were an item."

In the good old days when their bodies could keep pace with the rigour they put them through. "How well did he know Carole?"

"Fairly well." She sounded doubtful. "He hung out at the bar. Carole rehearsed while Ted tidied up, so Randall probably saw quite a bit of them."

"Think it's worth anything to talk to her?"

"I can't tell you if you'll think it's worth it. I will say that if Randall were in serious trouble and he couldn't go to his mother, he might go to her."

"What about to Ted?"

"It depends on whether he's still welcome at his home. Randall's burned most of his bridges."

"You have Carole's address?"

"Yes, it's on Pt. Richmond near Chevron."

I was on my way to the Richmond exit when my pager went off. I pulled over to the shoulder of the road and called the number which I recognized as Wesley Roark's number. Roark himself answered, distraught, feeling penalized. He had received a ransom demand on his wife. I turned around and sped in the direction I had come making the loop over 880 to 24 and exiting onto Claremont.

The traffic to 580 was frustrating, a slow wind on the mile. By the time I shot up Oakland Boulevard to the steep crest at the top of which sat Montclair's schools and fire department, I could feel his tension rising inside me, sorely testing my ability to ride the speed limit in front of the patrol car at my rear.

Mr. Roark's assistant met me in the drive. He was tall, blondish brown hair shaved, dressed in a comfortable tan sweater over a Geiko shirt and khaki trousers. "The call came in a half hour ago. He's frantic," Adam King explained, as we hurried inside the house.

Wes was pacing in his study. "It's Randall," he said, his voice tremoring. Dark shadows creased the skin beneath his eyes. "They want a million in cash. Unmarked bills. In six hours."

"Do you have the ability to cull that amount of money?"

"Yes. In fact a year ago the Board of Directors authorized me for 1.2 million with one signature."

"Who knew of this?"

"King, my secretaries, attorneys and the board."

"Did Genieve? Or your son?"

"Neither. I was instructed to put the bills in two airport carry-on bags and bring them to the Hyatt in downtown Oakland."

I consulted my wristwatch. "You have less than two hours before the banks close."

"Adam has covered the arrangements. A courier will take the amount from the bank and deliver it here whereupon I will bring it to a room I keep on tab at the hotel. You are not telling me not to make the delivery, are you?"

"How do you know they have Genieve?"

"The person I spoke to put her on the phone."

"How did you know it was her?"

"Well, she barely whispered," he conceded, unable to conceal his anger at being asked a question. "But I'm not going to take a chance on the possibility it might not be her."

"No, of course not. I wondered whether you had a password between you."

He shook his head. "She sounded terrified. Her voice became choked up." So did his. "I just can't stand by."

"Were you given any other instructions?"

"No FBI, no wiretaps and when I get to the hotel I am to go straight to my room without first checking in at the desk."

Adam King interjected, "Normally we go together; I take a room across the hall and he lets the bellhop know which newspapers to bring up, meals, to clear the pool so we can swim undisturbed, that sort of thing."

"I'd like to station a few people around the hotel."

"No, no one," Wes was adamant. "I won't even have Adam there."

CHAPTER 7.

I HAD A BIRD'S EYE VIEW of the entrance to the Hyatt. The hotel's narrow visage had been designed to obscure view, but from where I stood — on the top fourth floor of the plaza — I could see entrants quite clearly. The mounted scope took in the full pad including the revolving doors and the revolving credit that potentially walked in off the avenue every day.

I watched for Wes's automobile, a stately beige Mazerati. When it didn't arrive I radioed my contact inside the hotel.

"Room's empty," the retired deputy from the Oakland Police replied. Alan was a short man who blended into a crowd, or seemed indistinct in a hall. He was chosen for assignments which typically called for spotting a doer, usually for the African American businessman who brought contraband into the heart of the downtown.

"I've got posts at both ends of the hall on every floor," Alan added.

"They should've arrived by now. I'll check with traffic." I switched com lines. "Anything?" I asked, when I had Sky Camera on the line.

"I have him in clear view. He's just delayed is all. I have the tag in view too."

"Is this King?"

"That's his plate ID."

I didn't risk a return call to Alan. This was Oakland. The Tribune Tower was two blocks away, the IRS twin stations also a few blocks crosstown. The hub of the white collar grey suit conducted transactions to a tune of a million electronic and standard cable trunk lines inside Pac Bell's Inside Plant. If the deskman couldn't find the right feeder chip to determine where an electronic charge was broken, then finding one vehicle's whereabouts could prove doubly laborious.

I lit a rare cigarette and sipped lukewarm coffee. I wished to hell Wes had confided more, told what this was really about. Between my drop-in visit a few days ago and Randall, he must've had time to reflect on all the stale deals of the past and come up with a hypothesis. After all his inside line was on the international commodities market where insurrections replaced stability and government cabinets were replaced by United Nations designees at the drop of a hat, or a head.

Wherever Wes's problems were hiding, separation from one marriage had not completely shaken loose the debris that characterized buying and buy-outs during that segment. How many friends in his social circle had been affected? The Hauptmans had lost a son; Wes was well on his way to losing his. Perhaps the conglomerates of the Middle East had struck back by choosing to eclipse the sons of each successive generation.

After another ten minutes went by I checked the scope and found the entrance bare. I placed a call to the front desk and asked to be connected to Wesley Roark's room. The call went through. At the other end a man answered.

I recognized the voice. I slammed down the phone. I yanked out my two way radio. "Move, move!" I shouted to Alan. "He's not in the fucking room! Yasman Bolivar is inside!"

"Yas — ?" The line went dead.

I was yelling as I strode from my perch and ran to the elevators. "All men on deck! You're looking for an Argentinian, five foot four, dark wavy hair, skullish face, dark piercing eyes. He can climb through vents, shut down computer systems, climb ladders, double as customer relations. If you can, charge at him, trip him; Go, go, go!"

It seemed like a million years since I had encountered Bolivar during a routine check of the newly built stadium in San Bernardino. Two thirds of the police were at Morongo Basin for an in-service when this rat tried to take the cashier after a baseball game. With a backup from the Sheriff, Marguerite Gaia, chided for her unusual last name, I went aisle by aisle through the seats while outside a team of Mounties made sure no one emerged. We found Bolivar crouched in the shadows, the take stashed in a backpack strapped beneath his shirt. In the confession booth he clammed up, refusing to say who did the job with him while we awaited his attorney who bargained him down a few notches and got him released on an O.R.

I could feel the blood coursing through my veins as I took the stairs two at a time, swung open the door to the sixth floor of the Hyatt and ran toward Room 636.

I could smell the putrid stench of blood before I got to the room. It was strong, overpowering, ugly. It emptied into the hall like toxic ammonia, the result of a bloodshot canister of wrongdoings and shocking vehemence.

As I ran toward it my body rebelled. I saw myself moving slower, my legs like a pendulum approaching its peg, but in reality I knew I instinctively ran faster, fearful I had arrived too late to help.

The door was ajar. I pushed it open. The suite was large, wallpapered in a threadlike design with paisleys. A rolltop desk and a fountain pen and ink in a crystal caught my gaze. Adam King lay on the floor face down, dark fresh blood pooling beneath his back, soaking into the cloth of his pin-striped shirt.

I rolled him onto his back. His thin body was heavy. It threatened to pull away from my grasp like a recalcitrant mass. Immediately I saw the scalpel lodged beneath the breast plate, its dead-on accuracy having felled him probably in the instant it struck. Through the rip it made in Adam's vest, shirt and undershirt I could glimpse the soft white skin.

I felt carefully for a pulse at the neck. No vital signs didn't mean there weren't any. I slammed my palms onto Adam's sternum and waited, then repeated the motion, glancing up as a shadow crossed the body.

"Better send a team up," I said to Alan who had just entered.

Alan placed a stat call for a Medical Examiner. "Jesus!

Who the hell knifed him?" Alan asked.

"Bolivar probably. Did he get away?"

"No, he was caught in the lobby. Caused quite a commotion though. What happened to Roark? Where is he?"

"No idea. Better check with the mobile unit."

Alan did. After a few minutes, he rested the walkie-talkie on a lamptable and patted his pocket for a cigarette and match. "Car's still in traffic," he said, his voice straining with disbelief.

"We'll track it later," I said. "Looks as though we were outbid."

"Yeah," came Alan's listless reply.

"First his boss' son allegedly makes a demand, now this."

"Roark probably made a few enemies in his dealings."

"No kidding."

"Who do you s'pose knew about the drop?"

"Obviously someone we didn't count on." I stood aside as the paramedics rushed inside the room and in a bluster of motion checked vital signs, strapped the body onto a gurney, set up an IV drip and attached an oxygen mask. One paramedic rolled up King's sleeves and inserted several needles into the left arm to stem the flow of blood.

"Looks like a scalpel took a main artery. Perp knew what he was doing. We can't do anything more without life saving equipment. We're taking him in." And departed.

The coroner gave the suite a once-over. He was a Jersey man who had toe tagged the best and the worst. Blond, thin with thinning hair over a bald spot and doughy skin, Ivan Niles resembled the newspapermen he'd juggled schedules with over a twenty year career.

"Better do what you can to keep the flash bulbs out of this until you figure a perp," was his advice as he set down his black bag suitcase, removed his overcoat and rolled up his sleeves. He scooped up two vials of blood from the carpet, removed a centrifuge and spun down both vials, saying, "You'll be lucky if you can ever get rid of this smell of blood."

"You think Bolivar did this?"

"Oh, is that who that was in the paddy wagon," Ivan said, with a glance to Alan. "You should lock down the hotel the way you would a foreign embassy."

"The city won't let us."

"Order the hotel to do it."

"What I'm saying is if you can get a court order by telephone, do it. I don't have the muscle," I said.

Ivan gave him an amused glance. He used my walkie talkie to contact the air base situated at Hayward and explained the circumstances. He gave the person at the other end my telephone number. Before he was off the phone, the lights went off and the flashing light on the telephone went dead.

Ivan threw the cell phone to me. "You have the only working phone in the joint. You've got approximately two hours before the lobby doors will open again. Their electronics'll take camera shots of anyone anywhere inside the hotel. Including stairwells."

I gave a nod. I'd been through this routine more than once. "I'm going to need you to go door to door with me," I explained to Alan. "Just inquire if anyone's not inside who should be."

We headed out the door. Alan took the odd numbers. We jotted down room numbers for people who didn't answer our knocks to match against a master list of who had registered. It took about six minutes to cover each hall and about twelve minutes to canvass each floor.

Within an hour and a half we were done knocking on doors and returned to the room. Ivan had completed his work. On the coffee table were a row of vials some with dipsticks, some with colored fluid that stood in a wire cage. With the aid of the microscope he had run preliminary tests conducting several panels, cotton stick and flat growth cultures. From these he would ascertain what foods or substances King had ingested and match these findings with hospital-run tests or if he died, scrapings from the body itself.

"Any ideas?" I asked.

"He must've been shot through the gut first because there's blood in his urine."

"Why here at a motel?"

"The place is not that unusual. Lots of people are lured to hotels. My guess is he doesn't realize he got the wrong guy."

"My guess too."

A small crowd had formed outside. Inside bedlam replaced calm. Patrol officers held back a line of onlookers and cleared the way for the investigators and coroner.

A command center mobile unit had pulled alongside the curb. With high tech electronic scans they were checking the street and surrounding buildings within a two block radius for listening devices and broken connections. A panel of sophisticated surveillance monitors hooked by modem to hotels, banks and office suites.

Wes Roark's Mazerati had been abandoned. A monitor obviously linked to a street light silently recorded the goings-on surrounding the vehicle, as a tow truck pulled into position and its driver, a forensic specialist for the county, hooked the automobile to the tow.

Alan led the way through the noisy Pac Bell Central Office. The clicking sound of Ohms readers testing equipment dominated.

"What've you got?" Alan asked the deskman in charge of the electronics apparatus.

Greg Neff had worked for Pac Bell for thirty years and had retrained when the system changed from a wire system to a predominantly electronic one. "It's 50-50. We got a read on feeder cables to houses across town an hour before our 360 system for billing went down. I barely got that up and running before the bottle knocking sound of the testors you hear went high volume. Materials is down, so is Accounting. The oustide Office station in the Piedmont called in to report a cut cable. We've got limited staff; there's only so much I can do."

"You were trying to track calls made to Room 636 at the Hyatt?" I asked.

"That's what Alan asked for," Greg said with a nod. "The problem is halfway to being resolved. Now that we know which station was affected we can send a crew to check which feeder cables were cut."

I asked, "Roark himself was on a cell. Any way to assess what happened there?"

"MCI is controlled by the FCC electronically. All it can determine is time of day Roark's component shut down. It won't be able to give a radar scan as to where the intervening network is situated. It's like a sawed off shotgun; you can't tell where the shooter was."

"If we give you a number for a suspect can you rule out a cross feed one way or the other?" I asked.

"We can't, unless the cell is the same number as the inside line which it probably isn't. But if you come up with suspect information, we'll run a check on who's called any of the lines in the past two months and then run checks on those lines. In a few days we'll know a thing or two, but chances are if this Bolivar has had bad press as a thief he's not going to be the one who tracked an inside line to your victim."

It would do for now. I surmised with a hit on a man of Wes's reputation the parties had been cautious and probably had made few mistakes. Bolivar would prove an embarrassment and this would be the end of him even if he could make rabbits disappear and pull scarves out of top hats.

When it was obvious I would remain in Oakland another week I called Marion to come join me. His schedule was too packed to break loose for another day but he promised he would come the day after. He was eager to see the sights, and I promised that an inquiry notwithstanding we would take in a theatre show, the opera, a spa at Calistoga and a drive through the delta and lunch at Ryde.

A call to the Hyatt had come from a location within the wilderness of Canyon country. It struck me as the height of folly that young Roark would have made a second feeble attempt at blackmail.

But as I turned slowly past the road that led to Randall's small cabin I breathed relief. As the road sunk deeper into the forays of a forest, and the golden light struck the Canyon countryside at an angle causing grass and low cropped pinyon trees to appear starkly yellowish green, my relief turned to precognition. Someone had gone to alot of trouble to keep members of the Roark family in view and I suspected to keep them isolated from one another. The groupings of the past had not proven productive for someone, presumably the perpetrator of the attempt on Adam King's life. With or without trouble, because it was hard to tell what methods the perp had pursued, the members of a close-knit circle had wound up in different stations in life, closed off or shut out by new business partners, one generation opposed to the urgencies of the other, various people deposed or disposed of.

Here and there ferns and oak trees seemed refreshing as did subdued rose and apricot. The soil was darkly red and moist as if the angle of light, perceived as a warmth and a glow, enriched the normally sallow dirt making it seem dampened and thus more mysterious in color and texture. Distant silver glints of metal stakes gave off a sense of newness as crisscrosses symbolically covered the land like a net of wire over a slope that as I rounded the bend in the road took on the shape of a shellacked braid of loaf of bread. A flourish of oak trees, their darkly rich shapes more like clusters of wooden tokens rather than an abundance of copper or silver coins, fronted the road. A group of teenagers had chalk marked in brilliant salmon, orange, green and yellow colors numbers which read sideways, upside down, right side up and at angles, boxing themselves in as if in tattoos the length and width of a cement block extracted from the winding road. The oblong blocks of numbers seemed to represent box cars of a train and ran a quarter mile into the forested terrain which overlooked the ice cold, darkish blue reservoir below.

Visible as I made a next turn silken cobwebs hung from thin greenly encrusted branches. A waterfall trickled from an unseen source, its flow splashing at length over rocks, each droplet containing a rainbow. The day was sharply ascending, sunlight a good eighty-five degrees, the heat barely tolerated but for an occasional breeze. A thin veil of silvery branches barely hid the modern home. Triangles of glass tipped skyward from a wooden cacophony of decks and enclosures.

I camouflaged my vehicle in the brush. I expected to find the house situated on the flank bordering the road but as I stepped onto the property and squeezed through an iron grill gate, I saw the home was actually far back against a hill. I took a path that led through towering Eucalyptus and scattered oaks to a clearing in which was the grey wood house with dark red door and buttressed glass roof. To some degree it was typical Eichler, but the owner had expanded on a theme of wings and glass and it reflected a sprawling affair of decks and opaque glass.

"Can I help?" The voice belonged to a tall willowy Navajo woman who was neither attractive nor plain in the face but somewhat flat boned with brown piercing eyes beneath blondish brown hair. She was dressed elegantly in a rust colored raw silk skirt that loosely hung to her angular frame.

I showed her my county badge. "I am investigating a case. A call was apparently placed from this residence to my client. Do you reside here?"

"With my husband. By the way, my name is Joyce Haverty.

He is Cornelius."

"Is this your telephone number?" I read her the number of the call placed to the King room.

"Yes, it is."

"Are you familiar with this number?" I read her the number for Room 636 at the Hyatt.

She frowned in thought. "I don't believe I am. Would you care to come inside?"

"If you don't mind." I followed her inside.

The red door led to a courtyard of birch trees and a water-fountain comprised of slate and a bath of metallic pebbles. We walked through a second door into a living room surrounded entirely by glass. The backyard was small, a strip of grass with more birch trees and a tiered slope of moss and maidenfern. A modern sandstone fireplace separated the room from an adjoining kitchen, also surrounded predominantly by glass. The sink and stove were in an island in the center of the room. One black leather couch rested against a wall and faced the garden. We stood as she debated whether to sit.

Twisted metal sculpture dominated the long room. A rug made from a polar bear sprawled over a cherrywood floor.

"My husband is an artist," she said, and took me through the kitchen to a large room with skylights.

We sat on two plastic backed white chairs. On the walls were floor to ceiling scenes of outdoor wilderness spots in California. Intensely red redwood trees from the Highway of the Giants, a rocky seashore at Carmel, the valley floor at Yosemite showed her husband's preference for isolated still life as did the bowl of cherries on a sloping dining room table reminiscent of images described by poet William Carlos Williams and the red door curved like a broad angle shot taken from a street light.

"Might I ask who your client is?" she ventured, her voice throaty as a man's.

"I'm not at liberty to say, but a threat was made on a member of his staff yesterday afternoon."

She considered this. "To what location was the call made?"

"To the Hyatt in downtown Oakland."

"My husband has displayed his art there previously," she put out. "Is this in any way related to the castle at Pt. Molate?"

"You mean out near the Chevron refinery?"

She gave a nod. "The reason I asked is because my husband has a buyer for several Northern California locations and he has taken the week to take photos."

"I gather he was not at home yesterday afternoon?"

"No. He was last here Sunday."

That was four days ago. "Was anyone here besides you?"

"No, we have a daughter who's away at a ranger program in the Trinity. She won't come home until fall."

"Does your husband have a cell phone for your home telephone?"

"Yes. My cell, if I use call forwarding, is reached by our home phone."

"I was asking whether his number was the same as the number for his cell?"

"His is. Mine isn't."

"Do you know who his principle is for the work he is currently doing?"

"Her name is Genieve Roark. She wants these pieces for her husband's museum."

"Have you ever met her?"

"Yes. My husband brought her here to see his work."

"What sort of scenes does she want him to do?"

"She claims her husband has acquired original castings of construction of various sites with similarity to architecture of the University of California's stadium. She wants photo shots and paintings which reflect the type of community where these places exist. One is of Pardee Dam at Mokelumne Hill, one is of the original Calaveras Cement aqueduct at Mark Twain, one is of a cement gate at a park out near C&H factory in Pinole, another is of the front of Chapel of the Chimes mortuary, one is of Sather Gate, one of Temple of the Wings on Buena Vista in Berkeley, another of the band shell at Lake Merritt. There are ten sites in all. All have the same poured cement decorum."

"Interesting."

"My husband thinks so. He says the display will draw on numerous mason and shipbuilding communities in and around various ports including in the upper bay."

I said, "What does Mrs. Roark say prompted this interest?"

"Her husband has a home in Piedmont which has part of an aqueduct on its property. Since the Berkeley/Oakland firestorm of 1992 many original cement structures similar to Sather Gate were destroyed."

I wondered whether the parcel of land once owned by her family had anything to do with the interest. Perhaps she wanted to resurrect an old argument as a foil to new legal action to be repatriated for land lost. "Any idea how the display will be used after its completion?"

"We weren't told."

"How much is she paying?"

"Ten thousand." Then, lowering her voice, she said, "She asked my husband to produce several reproductions."

"Do you know of which sites?"

"One is Temple of the Wings, that I do know."

"It'll be an unusual post millennium exhibit."

We stood. She said, "Cornelius feels it will draw the Sculptor collection to the Roark Museum perhaps permanently."

"And make it an emporium for the gods?"

She laughed.

CHAPTER 8.

I ENTERED THE CITY MORGUE by the back entrance.

In the operating room a medical technician had emptied duffel bags onto sixty-five pound gurneys and was trying to determine which body part belonged to which of two bodies. I had watched San Bernardino's own county coroner Rand Teale sort through many a grisly backyard find to put together the correct bone fragments and matching ID photos. These bodies were no doubt the results of severe trauma and it would take several techs to sort through the collection.

I could hear the patient voice of a male deputy on the telephone triaging pickup times for the newly deceased.

"Date of birth? Time of death?" The deputy paused as he jotted the information on a form. "Who pronounced him dead? Is a paramedic on site? Where is the body in the house? Next of kin? Girlfriend's name? Is she living at that address?" Another pause. "Are the parents of the deceased living? Who is the regular doctor? When did the deceased last see him?"

I took a chair in an empty cubicle. I knew Michael Sinclair from my intern days when I knew Terry.

He turned to me. "It's been years, hasn't it?"

"At least fifteen, if not longer," I said, taking in Michael Sinclair's round face. "You look the same."

"I don't feel the same," and patted the beginning paunch that signaled the desk job was taking its toll. Then: "You look good yourself. What brings you up here?"

"Favor for a friend. Terry D'Coteur."

"How is she?"

"Doing better than we are."

"The socialites usually do. And you?"

"Detective, Oakland."

"You could've done Sheriff."

"I didn't want to answer phones two days out of the week. I wanted to handle the blind dates and the drug busts."

"Well, you could probably get a real post these days."

"I make out okay. I'm on an investigative team, I don't staff prison duty."

"There was a break out at Los Osos two weeks ago."

"I heard. So what's the lineup on your telephone call?"

"Oh same-old, same-old. Lady friend last saw her man friend at 8:00pm, she talked to him at 11:00pm and he sounded okay. She lives in a trailer park out in San Leandro off Fourteenth Street. She said he'd seen his physician a week ago for diverticulitis." He took the next number from a log and assigned it to the case.

"Do you remember a motel death on McArthur near Permanente about seventeen years ago?"

"Maybe. Refresh my memory."

"There was no sign of foul play. We couldn't send copy of death certificate to vital statistics because there was some screw up with the funeral home not accepting the burial? We had to run across town for the hard copy."

"Oh yeah, the guy who died of poor circulation. What about it?"

"Well, don't you remember the scar on his chest?"

Greg gave a slow nod. "I remember something, not that. Why?"

"It was touch and go for a victim with pretty much the same MO. Questionable if he would survive a lung puncture by a broken inverted rib."

"Actually I do recollect the guy. The ME assistant who picked up the body said he thought it was a puncture, but the reported facts of the case differed. There was no stabbing per se or buckshot."

"Right. How long do you think the victim lived?"

"I'd thought it was at least a few hours."

"That's what I thought. Any possibility you can pull out

the name of the physician who signed the certificate?"

"I can certainly try. Are you here in town?"

I gave him my laptop E-mail. "Oh and one more thing. If you can. I'd like to know who picked up the articles of clothing and such."

"You're not an easy female to please. Give my regards to Terry when you see her."

The dead man turned out to be a machinist from the Grand Island in the California delta. He'd been raised in a prune yard and set loose in the crate business at a time when the lumber mills were shutting down their yards in the foothills and in Napa county. A female had come to collect his possessions and had been the one to follow the body to the funeral home once a physician was found who would issue a certificate of death. Oddly enough, there was an additional snafu with the flowers not arriving for the funeral and she went to the Oakland estuary to purchase buckets of long stem orange roses.

Kathy Moriarty had no telephone and had no friends nearby. Her address said she lived on Grand Island near the Grand Island Mission & Spa.

The freeway to the delta was one of half a dozen blood alleys in northern California. After picking Marion up at the airport in Stockton, we took 160 through broad sections of farmland consisting largely of endless acreage of golden tipped wheat and charted the Sacramento River as it wended its way past Isleton and half a dozen tracts to Ryde, Thornton, Locke and Sutter Island. The golden colored bridge joined Sutter Island which was closed to cars. On Grand Island the levee road wound alongside a slough beneath low lying oak trees and apple orchards. The mansions were large California Victorians painted in white, staged by wide verandas, some half dozen stone steps, broad lawns and separate small garages. Life was low to the river, movie stars living amidst spa owners, the Mission & Spa decked out with Tuscany trees and Roman statues and fountains fronting its drive. Youth and the youthful rich spent long weekend hours on smaller, forty thousand dollar yachts, or in fiberglass speed boats, tanning sleek bodies and courting thin blonds whose husbands would one day run for state Assembly.

Kathy Moriarty was in her sixties, a widow to a dozen men whose lives stretched from the Valley of the Moon to the back-roads of Brennan Island. She would never leave her riverfront home on Grand Island, for it was paid off and reinvented with decks and arching windows and a boathouse. When the delta was unknown except to farmers and fisherman, she had purchased ten acres and stuck a shack with a guesthouse on it. Her city friends declined to visit and by degrees she converted the guesthouse into a tool shed and put a second story on the shack so that now at sunrise and sunset from anywhere in the house she could look to the water and see nothing but water without a single boat.

Marion waited in the car. Kathy took me upstairs into an attic shaped room made of cherrywood walls, skylights and glass panels. We sat at an elegant table from which she served tea in navy blue and white china with sugared cinnamon rolls. The wood walls and floor made the house. A small bookshelf designed in the wall and a closet of a kitchen which looked down onto her fenced in yard gave her the effect of being one who is content to breathe in the undisturbed island living with or without the men who had come into her life for some portion of it.

"He had been my first husband," she said, as we sat pensively watching the water. "He had an apartment off Broadway across from the park. How he was stabbed was a mystery unless he went for a late night walk after we hung up. But no one wanted to sign the certificate. I was afraid without a death certificate no home would bury him and I didn't want him lying there for weeks on end."

"Did you see him after he was dead?"

"Yes, I did. I was asked by the Medical Examiner assistant to make a positive identification."

"You went to his apartment?"

"Yes. I confirmed it was him."

"Was his full name Alex Keith?"

"Yes."

"Did they give you his articles?"

"Yes, and anything I wanted from the apartment."

"What did you take?"

"A comforter, fishing gear, a book of poems written by him, and his winter jacket."

"Any bank accounts?"

"None. He was too poor by then."

I knew from sorry experience that all deaths were triaged through a county morgue and it was the mortician who snapped the final photograph. The newspapers were given the obit information if the name given by the deceased friends or family checked out. If the photo did not match the given name, the county called in the FBI who then tracked down the name.

In this case the man's name was not Keith. It had never been determined whether Moriarty had lied or simply never knew her husband's real name, but sitting here drinking her tea I had a finite sense of truth. She didn't ask men if they were who they said they were. She took them on their terms and if someone showed up at her porch after her friend was departed, she had nothing to say.

"Who was your second husband?"

"Man named Cobb."

"What happened to him?"

"He died."

"When?"

"July 1987."

"What was the actual date?"

"July 3rd."

"How did he die?" I asked, half expecting her to describe

an accident.

But she surprised me saying, "Cause of death was unknown. One minute he was fine, the next he had stopped breathing."

"Was it here?"

"In the boathouse. I found he had slipped and fallen on the pier."

"A book of poems was found in possession of a high school student by the name Randall Roark. Did you give him the edition?"

"No. His name is not familiar. I did donate several books a few years ago. Do you recollect the title?"

"William Carlos Williams."

"Yes, that book belonged to my late husband. When he died I made a donation to charity. The store is located in Isleton."

We followed the road past an abandoned truck yard through wheat fields. In town at H and Sixth was a house with cardboard cemetery "tiles" which boarded up the windows, an empty slot for the names. At the corner on Union was a two-story brick structure with Law Offices written in gold letters across the windows. Down the street the Isleton Musuem, Johnny C's and three doors down, Casino. Across the street at the opposite corner a white brick abandoned structure with interior courtyard with sign that read, Posted Keep Out with yellow caution tape, a dip in the road. Glancing to the side it was possible to see that H Street bordered the wheat field. Looming behind the park the Isleton water tank, bold black letters on white.

I parked the car in front of Rogelio's, Pineapple Restaurant and Lee Bros. Dry Goods. Across the street stained glass store with squares, oblongs and door sized painted glass — beautiful colors, red and yellow, muted lavender, opaque blue, a wind chime with dangling beads of blue and green transparent glass. River Edge Cafe on the corner. We entered the storefront with white lace curtain with Used Books in glossy cursive on the window pane.

The air was cool inside. I spoke to the proprietor, a silver haired Asian woman with waist length hair. She identified young Randall, said he had come to the store with a young girl who wore her hair in a bun and was slender with a pronounced collarbone. They had come to the delta looking for shawls and bracelets and had instead wound up window shopping for wind chimes and artifacts. The girl was one of those lookers who one doesn't forget easily. The bookstore owner said she thought the young man's friend was sixteen, if that, and had a father who worked at Los Osos for the prisons.

"I sometimes moonlight for the ward there." I wound up their conversation.

"Perhaps you know him. His name is Soames Mao."

"Is he Chinese?"

"Yes. Half. His mother was Caucasian."

I thanked her. Marion paid two dollars for a book about Chinese labor camps in the 1920s.

We took a side trip to Brannan Island. The river meandered beneath low trees, some white sandy beaches. We stopped at a small landing where the water had put down the pier and several feet out the pier bobbed in the wake of passing boats. We came upon a strand of two-story wooden homes and small boathouses adorned by iron balustrades, long windows, ceiling fans, exposed wood on the ceilings and walls. Someone's rendition of New Orleans, about fifteen homes, some with windows boarded up, others their shutters nailed over windows, wheat fields in every direction as far as the eye could see. Too, there was a small fire station that had been let go. It was made of stone and had a slanted wooden roof, a path to it from the dusty road, an oblong, greenish white painted wooden box propped against it, its cover closed. Upstream the river split into a fork and the west fork sullied through bramble branches, vineyards and apple orchards into a sort of wilderness where in the four foot deep river stood large houses on stilts, three of them, white wood, windowless except at the back, with a small craft tied to one. Marion said they reminded him of a virgin summer and of the thickest forests that used to lay on the foothills not that many years ago when he was a mere seven or eight. The hills had been stripped and their nuded visages were wheat colored turned golden in the sweep of a low wind.

We got back on the road after a snack and canister of water, made a U turn and retraced Highway 160 back to Jackson Slough Road. The air was sultry and knowledge of having lived a good-enough life stayed, satisfaction and humor both alleviating stress that normally kicked into a chase. At the freeway 12 I shot over it to harbors and slips and boats. The water was darkish green, grassy land bordered the far side of the waterway. Owl Harbor was like any swamp harbor in the South. I passed Bruno Island and the three- and four-story homes of the nouveau riche and as usual found more than I thought there were of the careers to support the wealth, evidence of the rich in blondes and their middle-aged, beefy faced, pouchy husbands some ten years older. We eventually wound up where we'd wound up before, on a levee at the juncture of Brannan and Andrus Islands where larger boats and sailboats were temporarily moored, fishing lines dropped impossibly over the sides, gorgeous thin women sunbathing in strips of garments, their once handsome counterparts drinking proverbial beers and lunching it up under wide brim hats.

CHAPTER 9.

I FLEW INTO HEATHROW arriving a little after 6:45am. Donna Boswick, an insurance agent for the diamond Bank of Biddle in London, met me in the lobby. She was my age, tall, very slender with small bones, short sandy colored hair cut short above the ears, blue eyed, and dressed in a conservative white woolen suit with matching pumps and gold leaf earrings. We chatted on the way to her car, a small Pugeot parked in a short term lot. She had worked for the same firm for twenty-five years and knew everything there was to know about million-dollar diamonds from manufacture to production and appraisal. On the way into London she talked about a recent break-in to Brighton Rock for a theft of sixteen opaque oblong two by four feet glass blocks inside which two diamonds apiece grew until they were ready to be cut. Because diamonds were light and heat sensitive and could not tolerate light including sunlight, they were stored usually in rooms at a cool temperature with almost no light except for a thin strip of window situated high up on a wall. Their agents had covered southern England's machinist areas and tool and die cast shops searching warehouses and knocking on doors looking for any storage unit capable of providing storage for these blocks. Their lead agent felt the most suitable place to look was in an area where there were as many warehouses in a district as houses to increase the likelihood of evading detection. Single floors were considered best. They were still looking.

"The name Hamilton came up," she said, in a typically clipped accent. "He was with a team mostly young women back in the late Seventies who broke into our diamond bank and stole the entire strong-arm drawer. They entered in blue monkeysuits and then disrobed in front of the cameras and posed in their street clothes. A very brash group we all thought. We lost them in the subways, as usual."

"Who were they?"

"Six young women, all brunette and one blond, and two blond men. In 1985 they boarded a cruise ship and never returned."

"Was there a Genieve Smith among them."

"No, why do you ask?"

Her cell phone rang and she propped it open. The fields siding the freeway fell in rapid abeyance replaced equally speedily by narrow apartment buildings with terraces and stone two story institutions with columns or arched windows.

Donna listened intently, her thin plucked brows knitted in consternation before she finally replied. "I always tell them the question is not where is the airplane even though in recent years that appears to be all they are asking for. I mean, look, if your pilot really is stuck in a field, he has Map Search to help him figure out where he is, and if he actually has to meet up with that particular plane, he should have the route, so my advice is to just tell him the airplane is on schedule and not tell him at what altitude it is flying nor over what coordinates. Sure, you betcha, I'll be at this number."

She punched a button to sign out. "We've been experiencing some pretty duplicitous queries from alleged instructors since that disaster in France."

"I have a diamond procurer whose security was penetrated for off-site funds."

"Yes, you said so, storage."

"My guess is portions of the screen were removed without overall discernment capable. Is that possible?"

"You will note when you receive the original art frame that if the representative photo and its three-frame film strip refer exactly then it could be, but with most art there are slight creations that film does not pick up. Once a heist is thought to be begun, whether or not you enter numerous files, you must obtain the original frame."

"I would imagine there are people who have had access over the years."

"No, not likely, once secured with a computer size actual facsimile, it is only possible to look at that. The frame itself is not hung, not mounted and in this case shown for a month. It sits in its own vault."

CHAPTER 10.

TWO DAYS IN AND OUT seemed like a whirlwind trip, jet lag altogether delayed. The train into Paris was a dull dutch-looking three hour ride with no martini. From the station in the cab, the ride to the hotel was frenetic, dizzying and a blur of stone edifice, narrow park, posh restaurants, cigarette and magazine counters, department stores on tree lined broad boulevards. Along the rue Dominique down past the iron gates of a museum and next a prefecture, along Rue de Moulin traveling at rapid speed, fountains and galleries, the cab arrived in a well touristed square to an inside hotel. If not for a morning stroll through the arc di trompe and toward the glass birdcage museum of art, leaving aside a stunning remembrance of the Palace Louis the XVII Louvre, lit like a Cinderella coach at night, green lights spotting statues of famous warriors, the journey to obtain one art painting would have been tedious, even the staff descending stairwell opposite the windowed enclosed courtyard of oil paintings and stone sculpture, following signs through hallways all the way back to the Office where a diamond was being appraised for description and then on toward the small vault to receive the original verifiable painting would have been all too like trips to Alameda Naval for secured documents.

"Were I not to know your client had the Pink Topaz the security ought to have been virtually inexhaustible," she said, as we floated past Notre Dame, its cantilevered rib cage elegant through the top of trees.

Oddly the verse that accompanied the frame were love poems in the hand of Roark himself written when he was a young student.

VERSE

Rain pastes wind blown grass
to the window,
In passion I alone belong to you;
It's no erroneous basis
Intrinsic hope like any indulgence
Seeks only to be an enduring affection
With long considerations to staying harmonious –
Possession like the love it manifests
Brokers its own domicile,
Breath of one's immortal soul
Of one's inmost heart
Slakes like water over a spill.

The river winds its path
Through islands of mansions
Exacting a parallel of tilled fields
And high flood plain grasses
I've found the way home
Many a breezy afternoon
Tying the skiff to the jetty
Sailing through the back door
Into your moorings.
Futile to ask if you love me enough
When we spend every hour
Side by side on the couch
Ignoring the time
As years fly by
Reading Descartes and Hemmel
Strolling through the garden park
Arm in arm to the smoker's bench
Me with hat and cane
You with a see-through lacquered parasol
Tending to the mackerel twilight

A sultry moody wind
The circulating air flapping my shirt
You a more agile mother
Stepping out with your dapper man.
But for errant gusts
Of scarlet peonies
Which petals scatter afar a promising field
October breezes
Torment as a memory of your laugh
Sends me unconcealed grief
Of dissipating scarcity.

Where but of childhood
When entwined we fall asleep
I knew nothing yet of manhood
At my tender seven
I recalled only your loving gaze
Happy
Not a frown or complaint
Before sunrise when you rose
To prepare sloppy milk toast and coffee
I reached for you, my mother
And you tumbled to me
A kiss on my lips.

The shush of the lake's
Barely perceived whispers
I am still taken by calls
Of your beckoning, your summon
A rudder skipping lightly over water
Aiming always for the wind
That has shaped my school boy soul.

In sleep I am often lovesick
Capsized by a bad dream

I am forever falling for your shadow
Forever enduring a lack of words
For your life has shored me
With the permanence of a man
Who will know his own passion at the last.
Pink blossoms have fallen
Leaving the tree forsaken
In concert they have produced a snowfall
Of long grown, often cut ground cover
To fashion an orchard
That construes no lack of attention
Because it stands as fruitful as the day I last saw you
A thousand cherries a crate
Ready to go anywhere
Their blossoms always as they descend
Piling up in slow motion
Careless of the consideration
Of wind.

Before we danced
I had a primordial
Knowledge of you,
I dreamed you
And each day you appeared
I would say I knew you a lifetime
I knew you as well as you know yourself
If I grieved you as I knew you
I was not yet aware myself
In some basic unfulfilled need.

The sound of your labored breath
Coming from your room
Strains for love's sake
I am forever close on course.
Breath comes fast

When caught,
Love is held –
The way we climb stairs
Pausing at every landing

I've instructed myself
To your inducements
Longed for you to return to me
In every corridor
Where Ancient Life calls
In cacophonous echoes
Like reoccurring imprints
Of waves washing onto the shore.
A son's love is itself an imprint.

My rib aches
I adhere to you in prayer
All relinquishments of death
Are vital supplications
I release like one who has mourned
The depths of sorrow

Every weekday I see her
Walking in the wee hours of morn
Down a tree lined road
Wearing a cape and tall boots
Lanky, measured strides
A cap over her brown curls
As she passes church wineries
On her way to the hospital
The sickly scent
Of hibiscus ever present,
A descent of ravens
Hundreds of them
Cloak the hills

As I rise from bed
My first love sleeping on her back
The baby on my matted chest
All promises surrendering me
To the enticements
Of new fatherhood.
Had I but in your arms traveled
Wide open continental plains
Oceans and shorelines
I've come to the boat of my affection
Dreamed far off dreams
Awakened port inclined
To your gaze.

In a moment of profound insight
As you waken to the rasping sound
Of the phonograph
As you throw on your dark blue robe
Pass through the door into the library
I am at peace in a rush of tranquility
To know while you read
Before daylight breaks
I may take an extra hour
Until I have to tidy up
For the arrival of our young son,
Your sister Lisa with four divorces to her thirty years
And her husband Sartan who for thirty-seven years
Never married despite the best intentions
Bring us figs and melons
Fresh goatsherd bread, pate, currants
Omelets soufflé, smoked salmon, corn chowder
Because we are nursing youngster,
Odd we permit them to stay all night
Talking

At lunch we bring on the gifts
Knit scarves, tweed jackets, Picasso prints
Venezuelan wall hangings
And send them on their way
Two days hence
Two indecisive photographers
Whose scenes catch love in a glimpse
Each a little like youngster.

I will always return
Like petals open
I will try to reveal my deeper shades
A hibiscus turns madder red
I become imbued with seasonal ripening
Until the sweetest most vivid tension
Stirs with obsession
Fuchsine annotto
Which for every remembrance
Produces more reciprocity
A divine awe
An unfeigned avowal –
Reluctance subsides into remission
The hibiscus closes in nocturnal dark.
If
Intimacy is a form of yielding
Or recomposing
A constituency of adjudications
Winter dispositions must find loss an abrogation
Summer latency its own persuasion
Pomegranate an abundance
Each seed a sweet consummation
A hundred seeds a unforgetting delirium
For in any language of confession
Surrenders, sometimes credible
Possibly humorous

Unrestrained, fierce
What I realize about Life
Are my wish for endless unendings.

The fan whispers
It is a cloudless day
An unpleasant visitation of heat
A febrile unquiet
Engendering a propitiating restlessness
We are repressed to one another
It is the exposure of the day
This languishing unresisting
A week of lost sleep

An impatient continual stirring about

Where is a cool respite
If not on the back porch
During a summer downpour;
Who will know where tranquility
Has escaped to?
If
We don't sit mildly tolerant
To petty annoyances
A fidgeting irritation;
This malaise of sticky heat
Hoping that the tempest will eventually abate.

Only under option of surrender
Must I place
If too brief a breeze
Gives relief,
All one may see
Is a boy with a kite

Who chases girls
In
Lilac evenings
When the neighbor's young children have wandered home
Grimm's fairies tossed onto the shelf
Mache, sequins and paint put away
The pathos of the hours extinguished
Imbued with infective endurance
Quieted to stillness, calm
Youth has dispensations – were I
When we were young
To have trembled breathless in your arms
Meltingly feverish
Trembling more than passion could bear
I could not have waited the day
To an obsolete prescription
Feared senility;
The past fashion of youth
Age a glacial vesper
A mellow seed ripened past its prime
Into veteran gaff, fallen beyond
Venerable age
Sudden
Unanticipated reduction
That surrenders more capable men
To feeble dotage
In fact I sit close to the window
Staring at the star studded sky
A memorial candle on the bureau
In a dormant state
Unable
To connect
I am surely deprived
I am susceptible
Of which indifference is the imposter

For emptiness,
Endless hours
The quiver of the lips, tears unbidden
Worn tossed leather gloves
Beside the tray with the mail
My life cast adrift
Comforted by the ceaseless spring
Of the fountain in the patio
Removed from life
Aged in spite of middle years
Closeted, while through the door
People call at me, talk and laugh
Their chatter distant
My attentions
To things demanding
The shores of my household shorn
This limitation too impossible to traverse.

I escaped my life when I traveled west
Took off the moment I could get away
Far from any real communication
Carrying you with me for all intention
I went in search of you,
Had you lived you would have been
At home
Cooking crepes with peach
Sweeping the floors the improvements to the library,
I placed a letter for you at the wailing wall
Sat on a camel at the pyramids
And smoked hashish through a water pipe
Paid passage
Across the Mediterranean
To lose the sense
That you have gone.

Thus,
When in the winter of springtime's past
When to the wine press crates of grapes have gone
Long after sweetest blooms have closed their buds
I will have seen your vision waning last;
The lark shall sing at azure pink dawn
The eclipsed moon a breve of life now done,
While Tradition a tendril chrysalis
Your prime run through wilderness a fawn;
The vernal equinox depleted of store
On wings of curfew's evensong death falls
In cold advance it shrouds my plaintive calls
Until the beating breath can beat no more;
 October's premature dewy morn palls
 Ill winds fly hastened to the darkest squalls.
The ideal of lasting love assumes
For every summer tempest of joy
A man's affection brings dearest late blooms
And windy skies shower sweet lease employ,
The female takes as her companion dear
Spontaneous discourse and playful wit
Verse and bliss and kindest works to hear
As much a merriment affectionate
In spoken ways the son adored does praise
The moon completes your descript aware
For ingenuity verses amaze
For laws doctrines exalted love compare
 Permanence learns from agreed consent
 Deference its reverence gives sum content.
I would always
Recollect
Pink snow blossoms
Staining
The ground piteously.
Even without mild occurrence

Trees from a distance
Seemed
Antlered deers
In a flurry;
A glimpse of the lake
Where only a cabin was lit
Borrowed on moving branches
A countless number of deer,
At daylight not a one found.

When I came upon Monterey
To the mission, cannery and sea wall
I rather thought as I sipped Burgundy wine
Gazed at seals swimming
There was an abundance of monarchs
Like barnacles on moss-indentured rocks,
I rather thought as I picked dried starfish
Off white cigarette sand, I'd marry
And when the tide rushed up the incline
Pulling garlands of sea weed horns
Smelling of salty air
I would finally make you
An honest woman
Because you are
My only child's mother,
Let me say
We walked miles along the beach
To marshy inlets
Where we would listen to the tide
Pound beneath the sand
Beneath our feet
Where a nesting ground for pup seals come to mate.
Cobble alleys, gallery and notaries,
Bed and breakfast flats and paintings of ocean
And reticent oils of a perfection of roses,

But for the lugging sound of the ocean
Floor spilling moonlight
I listened for footsteps
To indicate we were not the only weekenders.
It is during moments of Life
One lands on dancer's toes.

However he had implemented the verse as that mechanism which defended a single oil painting done entirely in blue, almost black, of houses at dusk, was unknown. The obvious answer was that Roark had shown his son how to work his security system, who but Randall would know what the structural coding of the screen on the console actually was.

CHAPTER 11.

COLLUM'S MODELING SCHOOL took up the top floors of a large renovated poured cement art deco building on Grand. A few doors down, a shiny red Cadillac competed with discarded ice cream bins for curbside space. Across the street, some Mexican boys in muscle shirts and black pants waited for the bus.

The neighborhood looked to be a hodge podge of black, Chicano and poor whites, with a sprinkling of law offices filling the gaps between the five-and-dimes and liquor stores. The elevator was crowded with teenaged girls who peered through long bangs. They were all blond and fair skinned and pretty. A young woman with red curls to her shoulders and a bright pink sweater and black stretch pants handed me an application when I walked into the front office.

I handed it back to her. "Investigator. Documents. This case is a private matter, however. I'm looking for a young woman who took classes here who knows a young man by the name of Randall Roark. Could you ask around for me?"

"Certainly. Do you have a description of her?"

"She wears her hair in a bun and has distinctive looks."

She mused, then laughed. She was a looker herself. "We have a few girls who match your description. Want to come with?"

"Sure."

We walked down a long corridor with shiny marble tiles and black varnished frames black and white photographs of ballet dancers in various poses and costumes. Tiny overhead lights shone from the ceiling. "Too bad you don't want to teach dance here," she remarked. She was thin from her collarbone to her waist, twiggy in the arms and wrists, her hip bones jutting through her tight pants. "My students would love you. I find they try harder when there's a professional to do poses for."

"He's a man," I said, taking note of a forty-fivish man in

powder blue pants and a white T-shirt.

"That's not a man," she said. "That's Sebastian. His wife owns the studio. Her grandfather took the business over from the Mathins when this studio was first built in the late 1950s."

"Yikes. Are you listed as a landmark?"

Passing a studio inside which a row of twelve ballerinas practised toe movements, I was struck by their faces deep in concentration, some pained.

"Yikes is right, and yes we are. Here," she said, and at the end of the hall, opened a door and we walked out onto a classroom beneath glass panes that looked onto the sky. Young men with short hair in proverbial tights held ballerinas by their bony waists as girls in pink leotards and dark flesh tights twirled.

She pulled a young woman from the exercise and spoke to her. The girl looked at me. She was innocent the way young girls in their teens are before they have discovered the ways the world can corrupt. Her skin was flawless, her eyes a large soulful grey, her face contorted by bones, a long neck and surprisingly angular bone structure at the neck. But for her reddish hair which this morning hung in a long scarf, her presence was at once uncomfortable.

"My name is Veronica. I was Randall's friend."

"Did he take you to see Kathy Moriarty?"

"Yes. He also bought me a book of poems at a bookshop in Rio Vista."

"Might I pull your student out of class?" I asked.

"It's fine with me if it's oaky with Veronique."

The girl blushed at the reference to her nickname. "It's okay."

"You can use Elizabeth's office." She took us to a room situated at the backside of the studio.

It was white with white moulding in the form of Ionic tops. A wood stand with a leafy fern stood in the enclosure of windows which stared down at the street. Bookshelves lined one wall. A large desk and high backed chair sat elegantly on an

Oriental carpet which was positioned in the center of hand-some hardwood floors.

The woman who brought us said, referring to a miniature stage of the Greek Theatre in Berkeley that rested on the desk, "Elizabeth has been trying to bring in a New York model but there are all sorts of complications. We've been asked to perform summers after photos of the new backdrops are complete." And then as if her explanation was insufficient, she added, "She has turned up photographs of older sites which when completed will enhance our concept of the stage."

"Is there any possibility you could arrange for me to meet your principal?"

"You betcha. I'll have her number when you leave." She closed the door softly.

I eyed the young dancer. "What is your full name?"

"Veronica Estelle Meek."

"And do you live with Randall?"

"I reside next door."

"On Parnassus?"

"Yes, at 4339."

"How did you meet Randall?"

"We attended Oakland Tech high school together."

"I thought Randall went to a private school."

"Not in eleventh or twelfth."

"Are you still attending high school?"

"No, I graduated this June. I am a month older than he is."

"And you chose to major in dance?"

"Yes. My goal is to dance with Alvin Ailey one day."

"Will you be part of this troupe?"

"Only if Dr. Dermott approves."

"Who is this?"

"She is the owner. That's her name. Elizabeth Dermott. If she feels I dance well enough she will ask me to audition."

"Will you be dancing Greek tragedy?"

"Yes. We will be doing Euripedes and Sophocles."

"Did you and Randall have a falling out?"

"No. He wanted to shack up and I told him I wasn't ready."

"How long after did he split?"

"Maybe half a year."

"Who did he go to?"

"Her name is Jane Hart," she replied. "There was another girl between us, or that's what I thought. Her name was Roberta Klee."

"Are both these girls at school?"

"Roberta's a dancer like me. She was the one I told about breaking off with Randall. I knew she thought he was buff. She went to bed with him, believe it or not."

"What did you think about her doing that?"

"Well, I was the one who broke off so I couldn't really complain."

"But it must have struck you as awfully fast, and insensitive."

"I was really surprised. I didn't think Roberta was like that."

"Are you and she still friends?"

"No," she said, and smiled. "Dr. Dermott put us in the same act in Midsummer Night's Dream. It was awkward at first. But after a while it didn't seem to matter. I just ignore her."

"Good for you. And this Jane Hart?"

"She's a gardener. She's really talented. She used to work in the neighborhood doing people's lawns."

"Any possibility she met Randall that way?"

Veronica shrugged. There wasn't much to her; she was thinner than I realized. Thinness was the style among teens nowadays and they wore short skirts and skimpy tops to show off their lean, trim bodies.

"Randall's dad hires someone full-time. His name is Sam Harr."

"Could he have seen her working, do you suppose?"

"I don't know."

"Did you meet any of his friends?"

"I met the Hauptmans in Marin and the Holyers out near

Mill's college."

"Anyone else among Randall's friends?"

She frowned as she thought. "There was a woman whom he said was his mom."

"Terry D'Coteur."

"Yes," she answered happily. "She was nice. She asked me to stay over one night but I couldn't. I had to be up early for dance class. My dancing comes first."

"That's the way it should be."

"Will Randall be okay?"

"Why do you ask?"

"He used to tell me things that didn't sound quite right."

"Like what?"

Veronique pursed her lips together. "He talked alot about going south in his car maybe to Santa Barbara or Ventura. He said he had friends there who were willing to take him in and find a job for him."

"What's wrong with that?"

"Well, nothing, but when I asked who these friends were, he always clammed up. One time I succeeded in catching him off guard and he told me they were a couple who had a house on the beach. I didn't believe him so I followed him when he drove to Ventura. He stayed with someone who lived in a rambling shack. It wasn't much of a house. He didn't talk to me after that."

"Maybe he saw you there."

"That's what Roberta said. She said I was a dog to have followed him."

"Would you remember how to get there?"

"I might if I were driving, but I don't think it'd make much sense on a map."

"I'm going south this weekend."

"I wouldn't be able to leave. I have rehearsals"

"Give me your phone number."

She did. "I can't miss anymore of my class."

I thanked her for her time and went in the reception area with a thin blonde who looked to be in her late fifties.

"This is Elizabeth Dermott," she said.

An attractive brunette in a white shirt and pants and a navy jacket with gold trim turned to me, her hand outstretched. She was medium height, blue eyed, well physiqued, confidant.

I took her hand. It was soft, the nails were manicured. "Deputy District Attorney Lenny Cliford."

"I thought perhaps you were working with the Oakland Police."

"I'm handling a private matter for a client. I am in communication with two Oakland Police officers, Detective Brice and Ames."

"Good man. His wife's a detective too. Have you met her?"

"No, I haven't socialized with him."

She said, "Well, I know they're a busy work force and put in a good deal of overtime as a result."

She steered me by the elbow to another office, this one a small conference room. The room like the other had the same wood moulding and hardwood floor but the window was oval and faced the back of a building. Pedestals supported vases of white carnations. The dark cherrywood conference table had ten chairs. Paintings of abstract designs were at once soothing and riveting, suggesting she used this as an orientation for funders.

We sat, she at the head of the table and me next to her.

"I understand you will be performing Greek tragedy next summer," I said.

"It depends on a good many things. I'm conducting a talent search for a diva in New York."

"Do you know the New York scene?"

"Fairly well. I'm a model. Ever heard of Silky Hair? They used to be a stiff competitor of Bright Lips and Ultra Care. I was known as the Silky Hair Girl at nineteen. That's almost forty years ago," she remarked, and threw her head back and laughed; whimsical with brains.

"Did you start this studio on your earnings?"

"It's a fair question. Many do on less. No, I inherited the studio from my father after he went to live in France. I was modeling and had a contract with Mascara which I dropped after my father sent me plane fare home. My husband is the dancer; he's the one who operates the studio."

"Who will recommend the dancers for the tragedies?"

"Oh, I will. No one takes my place."

"I understand you have a photographer for the backdrops."

"Yes. His name is Eliot Averty. He's an artist actually, lives with his wife in Canyon. He started here in sculpture specializing in metal in Oakland and had a place in an Emeryville warehouse."

"Know any of his other clients?"

"Not a one."

"Averty was commissioned by a patron to put together a demo of pieces from which your stage may eventually come."

"You'd have to inquire as to the nature of his contract with said patron. If she did not pay for exclusive rights, he can legitimately farm out aspects his contract does not cover. It's done all the time."

"Do you have a patron list for your school?"

"Yes. Are you wanting to learn whether I know this other Averty patron?"

"I am."

"Not a problem. I will get it," she said, and excused herself.

In her absence I browsed for a second look at the framed paintings. The abstracts were wistful, melancholy art that reminded me of Genieve Roark's work, detachment, sense of loss, ephemeral beauty were present in these pieces.

Elizabeth Dermott returned with a thick card file which she gave to me. The pages were cellophane and made for photographs. I flipped through photograph sized cards with the patron's name, address, phone and interests. None had the names Adams Roark.

"Thanks," I said, and slid the file to her.

"Anything else I can help you with?"

"I was wondering who the artist was?" I asked, about the abstracts.

"Do you like them? He's a little known artist by the name of Daimler. My father knew him, bought everything he could get his hands on."

"Ever heard of a man named Adams Roark?"

"No."

I thanked her again. If a school of artists had existed in the fifties when Genieve's father Adams Roark was painting, it wasn't known to her.

I waited for Roberta Klee to arrive. Like Veronique, she was tall and thin, yet dark with curly hair to her shoulders. She dressed conservatively in all grey — penny loafer shoes, pleated box skirt, black and grey striped top and a tailored jacket with lace around the collar and cuffs. Unlike Randall's former girl-friend, she was all smiles, a pleasant inviting personality.

"That's Roberta," the young man who promised to point her out said, flagging her down. "Hey Bo Bo, lady here wants to ask you some questions."

"Hi, I'm Roberta," she said.

"Lenny Cliford. I'd like to ask you a few questions about Randall."

"Oh, sure, I'm up for it."

"Can we grab a cup of coffee?" I asked her.

"That's a really terrif place," she said. With a nod she indicated a delicatessen across the street.

We hurried across the busy street careful to avoid impatient drivers. The restaurant was one of these artsy closet spaces crammed with black Formica tables on a sandstone tile floor surrounding a stainless steel island. Small lights gleamed down on smokeless chatter and soft speakeasy camera stills of fog and Lake Merritt. We took a booth with a window and ordered two espressos.

"I'd like to talk to you about Randall."

"Yeah, you said," she replied, and tossed three sugars and cream into her demitasse. "Well, I met him at Sebastian's. This other girl was going out with him, see, and when she broke it off with him I got his number and called him up and he said, wow, let's go out. He showed up in this really cool mint green car, all white wheels, and opened the door for me and everything. And kisses? What an amazing guy. After that I couldn't wait to go riding in his car. He picked me up every day."

"Why'd you stop dating him?"

"He stopped. He said this girl he used to know was back in town. I think he left me as a favor for someone else but that's just my opinion. I mean, why would he want to leave? I was having a good time, I thought he was too."

"I don't know, Roberta. It doesn't sound well thought out to me."

Tears welled in her eyes. "I really liked him. He was cute and sexy and smart. Most of the guys around here aren't that smart."

"Did you ever meet any adults he knew?"

"One. He took me to Los Osos to meet this guy. A really nice person. We stayed for a few hours. The man made us salad with warm mango sauce and lamb stew and we watched the sunset from his house on the beach. Then Randall drove home. I fell asleep in the car."

"Do you remember the guy's name?"

She shook her head. "He was a painter."

"Of houses?"

"No, he was an artist. He was really good, better than what you see in stores."

"Was his name Daimler?"

She smiled at the pronunciation. "No."

"What about Adams Roark?"

She shook her head.

"How about Averty?"

"No."

"Do you remember his name?"

"Well, that's just it, I don't. I'd like to, though, for you."

I tried to be helpful. "Did he show his works anywhere that you're aware of?"

She shook her head. "He's French I think, or at least he looks French. Medium height, dark dark hair, dark eyes."

"Age?"

"How old are you?"

"Forty-eight."

"God, how awful. He's younger than you. Maybe forty. He was a friend of Jane's, or so he said."

"Did you ever meet Jane Hart?"

"Randall brought her over once. She'd gotten pregnant by some guy and she'd just had the baby."

"Why did Randall bring her to meet you?"

"He said he was going to move her."

"Did you see the house?"

She gave a nod, took a sip of coffee. "At night, in Canyon. It was nice, although," she said shrugging self-consciously, "tiny."

I shared her opinion. "It is small. Did you ever stay with him at that house?"

"No. We did everything in his car."

"Thanks, Roberta. Take care."

"You too, Mrs. Cliford. You take care too."

I watched her walk to the dance studio entrance. She was the friendliest of the two and I sensed Randall hadn't worried much about her. The pleasure comforts were there for the taking. I was fairly certain Randall hadn't left her in order to do the right thing for a girl he had gotten pregnant. Yet, as I drank the last of my coffee and paid the tab, I had the sense that Randall was handling a job for someone and that disclosure was the very thing he had to guard against.

CHAPTER 12.

I DROVE TO TERRY'S HOUSE.

"Any news on Randall?" she asked as she let me inside.

"I think I have a lead on him. But you'll need to bring in a private. The only reason I could use to delay is a suicide/homicide with entrails or a wife beating with hematoma and fractured X-rays. Without that I have to return to work."

"I know, Lenn. I didn't intend for you to stay this long."

"Terry, let me ask you a candid question."

"Anything," she said, and poured me a cup of chai tea and cream. "You know I don't hold anything back."

"I know, and I appreciate that. When Randall brought his girlfriend here — "

"The dancer," she said, interrupting. "I didn't like her, Lenn. She was so much more sophisticated than Randall. I thought in time she'd outgrow him."

"You didn't want to see him get hurt."

"Well, you can't blame me. In some ways he's very naive."

"What about his other girlfriends?"

"I've only met one other. The Hart woman. She's not for him either."

"What did she look like?"

"She's medium height, thin shouldered, brunette outgrowing what looks to be a perm, dressed fashionably in one of those long crinkly cranberry silk skirts and a yellow sweater with a dark red lace scarf."

"Terry, she sounds stunning. What didn't you like about her?"

"I thought she was much older than he was, possibly in her late thirties. I don't know, call it intuition, she knew too much about too many things, she had an air about her of one who has learned to make peace with one's shortcomings — something you don't get at a mere seventeen — and she seemed resourceful beyond her years."

"All good reasons to put up one's heckles. Did you know she used to garden for neighbors here?"

"Is that the question you wanted to ask?"

"Actually it's not."

"It turns out that in retrospect I remember her from times I had to see Wes before he married Genieve. She worked with a man for several of our neighbors, but if you're suggesting that Randall went into business with them — "

"I'm just asking. Do you know whether she may have had any knowledge of Randall's use of art for databases?"

"You know it's a possibility. She hooked up with Randall after he began staying with the Hauptmans. She could've been interested in Neil Holyer's collections. More than that, I couldn't say."

"What was Randall's original interest in Hauptman? Did he ever discuss this?"

"I know Hauptman had just changed his database, but I believe he wanted Randall to design some sort of artistic interface."

"Did he have any interest in Genieve's family? Her father was an artist."

"He didn't appear to, but then I wouldn't know one way or the other. He's been the most difficult since Wes married Genieve, but I chalked it up to a personality clash between them."

"Any possibility she discovered him doing something to his father's system?"

"Anything's possible. Why don't you talk to her? She can probably clear up questions about why he left, or if she had anything to do with it."

"Did you ever see Wes's system?"

"Yes. It's fairly standard. It has a special orientation screen saver — "

"Can you describe it?"

"It's a series of images packed into a small space. The strip of collectibles is actually an image of a shadow, it turns into aspects of images, then shows as a slot. If you manage to intercept it, you find yourself inside a field usually an oil or landscape which has as a background to it high resolution designs. Then he has dimensions to each image and it's backed up by verse. If you get these correct, you are inside the database."

"How come he didn't get offered a job? He's ingenious, creative, likeable."

"Actually he's very trying to get along with easily."

"So the Hart woman changed his outlook in some way."

"He's supporting her, isn't he?" She was bitter.

"What would he be doing otherwise? Working for Neil?"

"Or for his father. It wouldn't be the end of the world."

"What about Averty?"

"I don't know who that is."

"He's an artist who resides in Canyon not far down the road from where Randall lives."

"I don't know him."

I described Averty's wife.

Terry was silent as she considered the last of her chai tea. I watched her thinking affluence had gracefully aged her and allowed her pose and contentment which had she had to work as I or John had, she would have telltale lines on her forehead, mouth and eyes. There was a time in my youthful vanity when all my close friends were chosen in part for their agile beauty and when my mark of success grew, theirs also peaked. Now I had entered a type of mid-life known to law enforcement and the upwardly mobile blue collar, which many of my associates were, in which divorces and mid-life dissatisfaction and aging lines replaced the physique of one's enterprising years, robustness for long hours spent reading Jung and Spinoza before a fireplace wrapped in a woolen blanket.

I said, "The lead I have on Randall is that he's taken a job somewhere near Ventura for a security firm, but this is strictly conjecture. I think Hart got him the job."

"What kind of job is it?"

"I don't know. Maybe he's going after photocopies of Neil Holyer's collection before the pieces are actually sent to the people who have paid for them."

"God only help us. Why would he turn on us?"

"I don't know that he has, Terry, but it makes more sense than that he's gone after a cash cow of his father's estate. Aside from the million dollars stolen from King, the only way to cash out his share of his father's company's stock is to sell them."

"You think he had Adam set up?"

"It's the most likely explanation. Have you ever seen these two?" I showed her the two Bolivar brothers.

"No, who are they?"

"Hoodlums. They pull quickies, usually at stadiums, for large amounts of quick cash."

"I'm okay with you tracking Randall if Wes is alright with it. I understand there could be risks and that I might not want to know much more about his activities, but I'm his mother. I want to know what's happened. Have you asked Wes what he thinks?"

I thought Wes would say his son was in bed with the devil. Or that going after his son would be like chasing a plane down a rabbit's rectum for someone who'd crashed a small two seater into an Aspen tree.

But no one appeared at home. The lights were off.

I walked up the marble stairs that fronted the expansive colonial home. The door was slightly ajar. I pushed it open and entered the foyer. The air was cool. I groped for a light switch and finding none moved cautiously across the floor to the study. I found the light and turned it on. Wes lay against the armchair, his head thrown back unnaturally, his left hand slightly open. His clothing soaked with dark blood. A glass lay overturned on the lamp table, the amber liquid having dripped onto and stained the carpet. The carpet was still moist to the touch. Beside it rested an envelope and photo of his wife standing beside a man whose identity was unknown.

The thoughts that sprang to mind were unattractive. Wes had become targeted as a man who could move power pieces on a giant stage. He was an icon, a figure whose dealings had walked someone very imposing, frightening, into his most private of sanctuaries and decimated him. The Bolivars were at large; their South American contacts hidden in domicile shadows, wings of despots who but for the murders of heads of state moved callously through shadows of other demagogues, satisfied only with violent and cruel undertakings which left whole societies to reverberate in fear of their nameless personages.

I wasted no time. I called the homicide division for the police, then placed a call to Terry and told her to come straightaway

CHAPTER 13.

"I'M SHOCKED," TERRY SAID, turning her face into my shoulder to cry. "He wasn't yet seventy. Who could have done this?"

I comforted her. The police crime scene technicians poured over the entry and study. A young man in a smock dusted the desk and objects of the room. A woman with head gear used a laser lamp to detect footprints on the carpet. Another man followed her, at the ready with photographic paper to lift prints. I thought they were wasting their time, that there'd be no prints, let alone unusual powders or residues to indicate where the culprit had come from or why he had killed Roark.

The house felt empty despite the forensics people. I nudged Terry into the backyard where she slumped onto a patio chair, wits undone.

"It doesn't make any sense," she said. "Where the hell is Genieve?"

"I'm right here," came the stony reply from behind them.

Genieve stood quietly, clearly ill at ease, her exotic silvery beauty for the moment depleted. I took her in at a glance, her fair complexion, warm blond hair, sophisticated navy dress with ruffled lace on the blouse bib, and navy high heels. "I just got home. What the hell's going on? The police wouldn't let me near Wes. Is he okay?"

"He's dead." I had a mean sense of her having rehearsed this scene a handful of times such that now as I stood to help her into a chair and she fought me off and remained standing, if somewhat rigidly seemed somehow exactly right, and also exactly wrong, stilted, not quite preserved to click with precision into place.

"Dead?" The word caught in her throat. "How did he die?"

"He was shot at point blank range."

"Why didn't it destroy his face?"

"It shot through his chest."

"Jesus!" She clutched at her neck.

Terry got up, walked inside and returned with crystal glasses and the decanter of brandy, and poured each glass neat. Genieve downed hers in a shot. She prepared to pour herself a second but Terry gave her hers. Genieve stared at it as if it were the sum of all things evil capable of cracking a fragile world, and drank it, bitterly, resignedly, without further expression, her face soldiering into an implacable design of incomprehension, or of practised containment.

"I was visiting the solicitor as to the sale of our summer home." She said.

"Where is it located?" I asked politely, at this point not caring whether the necessary details were tracked. Case in point would be sufficiently researched by the divisions of police represented by the forensic teams inside. I doubted if my mind — alertness thoroughly dented — was good for much of anything.

"It's in Carmel a block from the beach. We took one point four for the one in Malibu."

"A million four hundred?"

"Yes." She was dazed, assaulted by disbelief. "I had to meet my solicitor because Adam was unavailable."

"I thought Adam returned to his duties yesterday."

"He did, but Wes sent him home early."

"Is Adam at home?"

"He may be. I can give you the address. He has a room here, but he rarely stays over."

I gave her a pen and pad, and she jotted the information down. "Will you be requiring our solicitor's name as well?" She asked.

"Please."

She wrote his name and number also. "The problem is we all thought that because the alleged kidnappers placed Randy on the phone that he may have engineered his own kidnap." She gave Terry an apologetic look.

"We thought the same thing too." I said, cutting in, "especially since he became involved with the Hart woman."

"I tracked her down," Genieve said, more to Terry than to me. "I couldn't believe Wes had written this woman a check. It was outrageous. For all anyone knows the child isn't his. Even if it is Randy's, Randy should've asked if he were in need of cash."

"What happened?" Terry asked, as her partner Albert stepped onto the patio and came to her side. He was a reddish brunette with wavy hair, tall and broad with broad shoulders, a cute Jewish guy whose liberal politics gave him the upper hand in most discussions with physician associates whose ivy league upbringings predisposed them to playing the stock market and who purchased two houses, pricey cars, were inveterate wine consumers, skiers, flyers, bred for adventure, if not for steep living on steep ravines.

"I made it as soon as I found your note," he said.

"Sweetheart, it was good of you to come. You know Genieve."

"Yes," and shook her hand. Then: "Lenn, thanks for holding down the fort. Has Randy surfaced?"

"Genieve was saying she tracked him down," Terry said.

"Where the hell is he?"

Genieve said, "I went to DMV for his address information and obtained an address. It's in Atherton. A young woman there said he was staying weekends while working for a professor who works for AMES. I drove out near the airport. I told her she has no idea how dangerous Randy is."

"We don't know that he's dangerous," Albert put in, more in defense of Terry.

"I think he is," Genieve said, asserting her opinion in a forceful tone that left no room for disagreement. "Anyhow, she said Randy works for a Professor Sun on weekends transcribing notes onto his computer. This Sun is writing a book on aerodynamics and sound for NASA. I spoke to Professor Sun who is very impressed with Randy, said he paid him by the page for transcription."

"Did you talk to Randy?" Albert pressed.

"Yes. Two days ago. He answered a number Professor Sun gave me. Randy said he had his work cut out for himself and was doing his best not to involve us."

"Did you ask what he meant?" Terry inquired.

"Of course. He said he'd had a mammoth argument with his father who had taken something he said out of context and he didn't want to take another cent from us. I told him it was silly and he should come home straight away, but he dug in his heels, said he was doing fine and planned to continue as he was."

"Were you aware of such an argument?" I asked her.

"It was a long time in coming," she replied. She dabbed at her eyes. "I raised a son myself. I've been through the teen years. They get this idea into their heads they can do anything." Her voice was muffled. For a moment she tried to stifle sobs. Recovering herself, she said, "Randy really rebelled. Wes said he was Terry's son more than his and he was having a hard time getting Randy to come home, let alone confide in him."

"This is probably going to get tough on you. Is there someone you can stay with?" I asked.

"I have my family. My aunt has a condominium at Lake Merritt. I can go there if I need to. Or there's a cousin in Moraga who has a home. My son resides in Santa Barbara."

"It's ironic you just closed on your summer home in Malibu," I said.

"Yes, it is. Wes needed the capital and it was fairly useless."

"For what reason did Wes need the capital?"

"He was having problems with his museum. He didn't go into detail and I didn't press him for information."

"Was someone in charge other than yourself?" I asked her.

"Wes hired a man last fall by the name of Childress. For all intents and purposes he's in charge."

Officer Rick Ames poked his head outside. "The funeral home has arrived for your husband's body," he said. "Do you want to accompany them?" He asked Genieve.

"Yes, absolutely."

"It's Mountain View Cemetery."

"Will I be needed to complete arrangements or sign papers?"

"Yes, it's fairly detailed. They require your permission for burial. Or we can talk to your solicitor."

Her face took a quiver, the first sign of real emotion. Within hours, after she had gone through the motions of burying another partner and of discussing the fine print with her solicitor, hell would settle in, its sharper edge bargaining against a tide of remorse, apathy and stony awareness that she was alone. After that, guilt would come to claim her loss, and she would be obsessed that she should have been home earlier to prevent his death or should have taken him with her. The steps to reconciling death took up all one's psychic energies, borrowing on sleep as if on a limited account, prejudicial without outwardly seeming judgemental, a plethora of forgotten details that would when remembered rankle further.

"It's fine," she replied, trying to control tears. "I'll accompany my husband's body."

Then, to me: "May I speak to you in private?"

I went inside with Ames retreating to a far corner of the living room. Through the hall the chaps from the funeral home carried Wes on a stretcher.

Officer Ames said, "Small wound. 44 gauge, possibly smaller. Estimated time of death four o'clock this afternoon."

"Any idea as to size of chest wound?"

"Hard to assess without cutting away the fabric. Four to five inches in diameter, took lung tissue. He didn't have a chance."

"He must've been standing."

"I agree. He probably never saw the assailant."

"Any idea who was in the home?"

"Could be the wife."

"She has an alibi. Of course it will have to be substantiated. Have you checked for a break-in?"

"Not yet. Also we haven't checked his security systems, monitors, computer, so on. You staying over at the ex-wife's?"

"I live in Alameda."

"I'll call when I know something." Ames said. "You better send in a maid service to clean up. The household help won't want to touch this."

"Okay."

"Just so you know — we've posted an APB for the son and his girlfriend."

"Good thinking. You going to post a man when everyone leaves?"

"I'd like to but I can't spare the manpower."

"I'll call someone in. I don't want to leave the place unguarded."

Hours later over dinner of ravioli and marinated cucumber and tomato salad, after I had spent the better half of the evening dictating a petition for filing on adjudication for death due to suspicious causes, possible spousal interdict, less likely patricide by legal biological son, weapon 44 chest wound, estimated time of homicide afternoon, tissue described, spouse had alibi, I would tell John the case would never come clean now because there was no way to know exactly what Wes realized or understood in his final moments about the disposition of his son's kidnap. Whereas the petition would receive the Alameda County courthouse judge's signature sometime between nine and noon, would be filed by three the same day, my headaches would just be beginning. In the next forty-eight hours, my detective John would have to lock into place a street photo of a vehicle and person entering the Roark estate to define a killer, and a convincing piece of data such as a foreign fingerprint, hair fiber, or shoe print, and have a report on my desk for the narrative I would have to submit on containment on evidence. After that, it'd be back to the office to file fifty pleadings, after which would come as many investigative narratives as the D.A. had the detectives available to track suspects. The District Attorney office for Alameda was the battleground for all criminal handlings involving completed investigations, dead bodies lying dead inside someone else's house, child abductions, brutal domestic violence injury, stage coach robberies, drug loss relations, bungled murders, et cetera. Oakland was known as one of the worst morgue detail to work, if for no other reason the city mayor owned nearly all the funeral homes and the worst graveyard shifts consisted of male nurses on the take for powder grains. An average month for a sincere deputy was ten cases at the bench, most of which would wind up getting ditched for insufficient evidence or hearsay. In any given month rotation might consist of twenty tough teenage wards wanted for trespass or liquor store or department store burglary, ninety petty theft dealers, and a summer homicide. During a slow summer with one out of four cops on a seven week vacation, no cases were lined up, detective summaries took three months to file, and the court processed as many as a thousand divorces.

For now as I rode to the solicitor's home, I wondered whether Wes hadn't tried to financially cut off his son. It was not enough the young man had left his father's home in anger nor said harsh words he probably didn't mean. The worst was he had stayed away and in doing so probably hoped to inflict emotional damage and thereby bind his father to him in ways his father was not inclined. The fact of the Hart woman's pregnancy probably had not helped. Perhaps the original argument had had to do with her, Randy's career or worse, with an association that Wes refused to acknowledge for Randy.

Sylvan Reese was tall and bone thin, pleasantly aged with bluish white hair, a resonant voice, and a deeply thoughtful countenance. He wore a three piece suit that combined tweed and gold satin and a timepiece that he carried in his right hand. An aging barrister, he had accommodated everything from contracts to securities to clearances, and probably much more.

We sat in a sitting room which consisted of oak bookshelves crammed with books, two green leather couches, a grandfather clock, a writing desk made of glass and a time worn Kashmir rug over dark walnut floors. Two arched windows overlooked a balcony and a Victorian herb garden.

"I managed Mr. Roark's affairs for twenty-nine years," he said in a sonorous voice that left no doubt as to competence. "I've known both wives, given some pretty unsought advice in my time and am devastated to learn of my principal's demise. Absolutely astounded."

"Does he have a will?"

"Yes. We added a codicil after this last circumstance with young Randall. In short it says any young woman coming forward with a claim cannot receive a penny. It was necessary, Wesley felt, because when I ran a background check I was unable to find a Jane Hart with her particular information."

"What does the will say?"

"The estate is worth approximately three quarters of a billion dollars. A good deal of this is tied up in investments. A small percentage is liquid and can be cashed without much fuss. The first Mrs. Roark receives fifty mil. It's not much for all her trouble, but the alarming fact is her son is able to receive approximately a hundred million unless someone contests the will, and the majority goes to Genieve Roark with a modest portion going to the assistant Adam King. Mr. Roark has a brother in Denver who is eligible to a portion of the initial investment left the sons by their father. Then there are provisions for the key staff operations in the financial district in San Francisco, a dismal amount for the undersecretary, gardener and staff, and a list of charity donations meant to offset costs against the estate."

"How much does it look like Genieve will inherit?"

"A minimum of four hundred million, possibly more depending upon contests and fees."

"Roark really got taken."

"In my opinion he did not adequately respond to these recent threats."

It certainly looked that way, but I decided to reserve my opinion. "Any consideration given to interested corporate parties?"

"None. There doesn't need to be apart from joint ventures."

"Well I was thinking more along the lines that his wife may have gone into business with another party against his son."

Sylvan shook his head. "Nothing I know about. Now, if Genieve is found to be unfit for any reason, then the majority of principle is pocketed into an account until Randall turns twenty-five at which time he would be eligible to utilize it up to ten million each annum."

"What if any of this money was used to aid in the commission of a crime against Wes?"

"Then we'll no doubt be hung up in court for the next half century. What's on your mind?"

"I'm not sure exactly. Wes and his friends whom he knew prior to meeting and marrying the second Mrs. Roark were repeatedly robbed of high priced art and their security systems. These appear to have culminated with this ransom demand. There has to be something behind all this. Could prove to be something, or turn out to be nothing."

Sylvan rubbed his timepiece. "Mr. Roark's business practices are flawless. So are Adam King's. Neither wife had any access to use of his money on a grand scale."

"Someone gained access. Someone went to a lot of trouble to infiltrate systems, stage a ransom and kill Mr. Roark."

"It only looks that way. We don't know if these acts are affiliated."

Mr. Reese stood and I stood with him. Mr. Reese said kindly, "You've had a tiring and demanding day. You need a breather. Come back after you've taken a fresh eye to the same picture and have gathered some additional facts. Then we will speak again."

CHAPTER 14.

COMPUTER COMPONENTS lay spread across Lina's desk. She had removed each piece from its corresponding system for a look-see. None were damaged; when plugged into a test system the language emerged presumably undoctored on the screen. For a good two hours she poured over the information. With an interface she could decipher the tapes, pull out critical information and give the detective crew a byline. Information was cheap and chances were there were cannibals who'd infiltrated and seized passwords, docs and other vital information. Her guess was a handful of clerks who had outlived their usefulness in straight jobs had turned to black market ventures to turn a nifty profit. Every so often in most jurisdictions a slug would produce itself in random capture from a street camera positioned at doors. The government bragged about its high tech crime mobilization — not to mention the usefulness of singularly employed affirmative action recipients as wheel-powered tire treads who investigated children, parents and extended relations — religious and other groups spent money by the billions to invest in safety nets, and given the amount of donkeying these small gangs and outfits went after, it was money well-invested.

On a legal sized yellow notepad she had drawn a line down the center and written thoughts and impressions on the left. On the right she would create a storage bin of queries. These would describe findings as to Roark's stored information as well as holes in Detective Ames's narrative summaries which pertained to these components.

Her friend Max had taken off on a fishing trip and was due to be gone a full week. With him out of her hair, she would put in back to back shifts, mindless of dinner or sleep. Early in her career as a United States Marshal, Lina had thought since her partner, then of ten years, had grown up in Canada, they would eventually make tracks in that direction, build a home on marshland turf and raise alpacas or goats. In fifteen years she had vacillated between putting in for a supervisory position and retiring before age seventy and had for the time being opted for special assignments. A-team assignments placed her on a mostly night shift running interference for the sheriffs out past Apple Valley and Lucerne. Occasionally the feds called her and another marshal to the land fronting Sector 51 to patrol the fence, arrest curious thrill seekers and track satellites with special camera equipment. At her last 51 appointment a satellite had flown into a crevice. She manned the shovel light as a crew of twenty technicians took off the door and sectioned the flying machine down to its motor.

The initial Roark situation resembled a makeshift tent party that Sector 51 had utilized at one of its desert silo stations a number of years ago during tests conducted by the Coastguard of Aurora Borealis lights over the Colorado basin. Computers at the various substations had snagged a ghost ray slightly before dawn during early summer months. The Yucca Valley station weather system pinpointed the ghost at the trailhead entrance to Covington Flat and Ryan Campground. A thorough canvas unpredictably netted no results. Lina accompanied a detachment to the site at night and found light rays emanating strangely from the clusters of rocks closest to the rocketship-like well. When three homes were built at the base of the site the sightings mysteriously vanished.

She glanced up as I entered her motel suite and sat on the sofa. "You had a computer ghost," she said, when I was comfortable. She pulled the tab on a Dr. Pepper and took a sip. "Apparently it ate through a portion of Roark's files. I would venture a guess that his kid thought the problem was solvable."

I studied her with renewed admiration. If anyone could produce evidence of hacking, she was as good an analyst as any. She was slim, trim, five foot eight inches in stocking feet, blond with a few darker streaks, blue eyes and an unflinching attitude. At forty she was as sharp as the first day she started the job.

I asked, "Can you build a chronology of what Roark went after?"

"I can, but studying the lot of these recorder boxes will take minimum a good day and a night."

"Did they outfit you with the one from his laptop?"

"Yes, and the one from his limo the day he was traveling to meet the Randall designation."

"Good enough. Let's eat. What can I order in for you?"

"American."

We laughed over jokes she told me about summer jobs spent identifying sounds from components which matched language gibberish produced onto a magnetic tape when a person tapped the keys of the motherboard of their computers. She had worked summer jobs, odd jobs, anything that gave her access to a databoard, at the telephone company, overseas, sound recording studios, telexes, old systems, new systems. The metal strips in roofs and walls in a pinch could carry sound of computer systems out the door and down the street.

Wes Roark had had a leak. He knew he was unable to get rid of it. He changed his hardware twice and then ordered in new databases every six months in efforts to preserve the confidentiality of the information on his system. He hired in an assistant, sent different programs to various sites, even accepted his son's help to eliminate the leak. It looked as though when Neil's neighbor moved in, the problem escalated and electronic doors were left standing open unable to be closed and Hauptman's sophisticated art, while temporarily effective, were repeatedly penetrated, prompting a series of database break-ins which were subsequently deposited at other sites causing the system to test as though there were an intruder.

Hauptman was the brain genius of Roark's ventures. He too had permitted young Roark to tinker with his system knowing full well any infiltration would be recorded and immediately transferred off site to another CPU. Oddly he had been unable to store large amounts over a hundred million bytes without at some point losing most of his information. As a result approximately eighty sites contained basic information consisting of budgets, domestic and foreign investments and commodity trade lines. A crash resulting in shutting down four or more sites found limited dollar access to various commodity markets within a forty-eight hour zone. This being scarcely sufficient, Roark was forever generating new subsidiaries which his larger enterprises purchased thus allowing him to juggle profit margins, close down companies or borrow against them.

It was after midnight when I went downstairs to the lounge and ordered several drinks. A white bald man dressed in an oversized pin striped suit played feverish jazz at a grand piano to a sometimes interested crowd. Judging by one couple who sat in the purplish light of a window seat the man was about to pull out his key chain and exchange his hand on the woman's stockinged leg for a ride home. Instead I conversed with the bartender about the rising cost of real estate in the Bay Area. We kibitzed about real property, estates, condos by the dozen, uptown, downtown, access to San Francisco, relentless love, reckless equations and by two, when the bar closed and had paid the piano player and rolled down the levolors, I walked onto Broadway and hailed a cab.

I got four hours sleep.

In the morning still tired and pensive, I rode across town for a meeting with Roark's assistant Adam King. I passed the boarded up Sante Fe restaurant on University to Shattuck, took a right and cruised down the street past a landmark Wells Fargo and Sees candy shop, past a wall of storefronts, the theatre, Mel's on the corner, the refurbished greenish Berkeley Public Library and shot up Durant to the Women's City Club. I parked in an underground lot and walked to the art deco building erected in the 1940s. Its wrought iron doors opened onto a staid lobby not unlike most hotels built to commemorate the Sather Gate area, comfortable old stuffed chairs, upholstered high backed twins, desks and antique long tables. I took the stairs to the mezzanine where I found a casually attired Adam King had begun breakfast of English Breakfast tea, fresh fruit-cup and scones with butter and strawberry jam.

I poured a cup of fresh brewed coffee and grabbed a scone with butter.

"I hear you talked with our barrister."

I took a sip. The coffee was piping hot. "Yes. Mr. Reese gave me the size and shape of the trust."

"Then you know I cannot possibly have had motivation."

"I hadn't considered you to have any. What caused you to ask?"

"Detective Ames asked that I come downtown to give a statement this morning."

"He probably wants to learn when you left — "

"I shouldn't have, you know." Guilt would make a poor substitute for grief. "Although I will say it was very much like him not to impose."

"Well you were recuperating."

"Yes."

"And I guess he was tired from the ordeal."

"He was. In fact, he gave the gardener and his wife's maid the day off. He told me he wanted to be alone to think."

"We always wish we had made a different decision in retrospect. Perhaps if you had been present, you'd be dead."

"I hadn't thought of that," a somewhat ruffled King remarked. "Any leads?"

"We have one, but at the moment it appears to be a dead end. What do you know about Geneva Roark?"

"Wes brought in several firms to investigate her."

"Why?"

"This was before he made an engagement. He wanted to know what her interest in him was."

"Do you have the names of these firms?"

King was one step ahead. He proffered a piece of paper on which he had written their company names and phone listings. "The second advised Wes to draft a pre-nup."

"Was she badly in debt?"

"I have no idea as to the circumstances but as you can see, he acted quite to the contrary. He practically left her everything." He sounded angry, although detached.

"Why do you think he did that?"

"The problem with his son left him little alternative."

"Do you find what happened with his son coincidental?"

Adam was cautious, a patient advisor who knew the limits of his influence. "It is possible he intended to change it but was killed before he had a chance to ascertain his son's involvement."

"It is possible. Did you know his son worked for a professor at Ames?"

"Then you've spoken to Randall. What does he say about this wild goose chase he led his father on?"

"He hasn't been found."

"You do know about the efforts he put his father to?"

"No, I'm not certain I do know."

"He wrote his father that he was staying in a small apartment at Atherton, then a month later wrote he was going to Monterey to research a new system, then a week later wrote that he had taken a brief job in Ventura and was given a small studio overlooking the beach. He said he was earning good pay and he'd be able to give his child a name."

"When did Wes receive these letters?"

"Several days after he met with you."

"Before the ransom?"

"Yes, immediately preceding. Wes finally sent the correspondences to a handwriting specialist in San Francisco. He suspected they might be forgeries."

"Who'd he go to?"

"Woman named Ella." He gave her her full name and number. "Wes used her in the past on other minor stuff, once to verify an art object Neil purchased."

"She must have some good connections."

"Wes felt she did."

The private was named Ella Charles and she worked out of a dingy closet located in North Beach near Fiore D'Italia. Her office was up a flight of stairs, down a hall in which sat two chairs, a lamp table between them with a small plant on it. A room which I guessed was thirty feet long by twelve feet wide housed a water cooler, a stand-up computer desk with a monitor in view, a sofa, two four-drawer wooden files and a large silver framed brown and white print of the Presidio. At the end of the room was a window with a wide ledge on which she had positioned an iron cat statue.

Ella herself was tall, pale complected, with a shock of short, red bleached brunette hair. She wore linen trousers with suspenders, a no-frills stiff collared shirt with rolled up cuffs and a red bow tie.

She had not forgotten the case. "No forgery. I told him that."

"Do you have a sample of his writing upon which you based your decision?"

She retrieved the file and made a copy on the fax. I browsed through the sheets and regarded Randall's signatures. The postcards were all recognizable. "No intent to deceive."

"That's what I said. Obviously his concern was could anyone have imitated him. As you can tell, these appear to be the genuine article. Roark said he was being bribed and wanted some idea as to his son's complicity. I told him I considered these actual writing samples. I asked him for sample demands.

That's on last page."

I flipped to the final note. It read, I think I'm entitled to something more than a pittance you toss my way every month. A thousand additional would be helpful. "When I saw him about a month ago he said he was doing fine."

"Perhaps he thought his father would comply."

"You ever meet Roark in person?"

"Once. A year ago. He came with his wife. She's a high maintenance type."

"I agree. Did you conduct a search on her?"

"Wasn't asked to. I did conduct one for an artist named Averty."

"How long ago was it?"

"Six, seven months ago, back in December. I ran standard checks, pulled up a history from DMV as well as credit, zeroed in on various establishments he frequented, took a photo to some, verified he was indeed himself."

"Did Roark want to know anything about computer capability?"

"He asked. I gave him Averty's uses of digital graphography including use of E-fax. Straight forward, nothing queer there."

"What would Roark consider a queer case?"

"Investments, certain commercial uses of light for instance X-ray or medical access. There was nothing. I think the most Averty ever went for was a two thousand dollar investment in Kodachrome."

"You have any familiarity with companies named Josephine or Litchstein?"

"Litchstein & Lake. They're right here, few doors down. They run standard profile concerns, make advisements as to custody, divorce, retirement, that sort of thing."

"What's their specialty?"

"They advise the millionaire as to potential for ambush."

"You're joking."

"Nope. We all specialize in something. That's their's."

❖ ❖ ❖

A party was going on when I entered through the luxurious opague storefront. Stylish women wearing glittering backless dresses and men in dark suits and white starched shirts mingled inside an adjoining room. High ceilinged white walls, blond hardwood floors, desks with Apple computers, memory and printers caught my view in the large room.

A man came out to see what I needed. I told him, and the man promised to send out the man whose account Roark had been.

"Police came out," said a young man who looked to be in his late thirties. Blond, good looking, white trousers, black shirt, white tie, white sneakers. He was John Lake and had been with the firm since it opened. "I was dumbfounded." He said apologetically about his principal's demise. "Wes was good to this firm, sent us lots of business."

I followed him through the jungle of desks and computers into one of three small offices at the back. A campaign ad that read Your health is a clean slate decorated one wall. On the opposite wall was a poster of a Muni car with: who carries you home? The office felt wedged between two ad programs like a bum prosthetic.

"Safety. That's what I handle," said John. "Every account imaginable. Health care, city crime, cigarettes, child abuse. You name it, I've done it."

"It certainly has its effect."

"It's supposed to. These campaigns are requested by politicians."

"You ran an investigation on Geneva Roark."

"We did." He gave a face. "She's an interesting woman. She's lost every husband around July 4th. I used a private investigator out of South San Francisco who said he couldn't put his finger on it but thought something was definitely wrong."

"Maybe it wasn't coincidence."

"You think this isn't coincidence? This is two weeks past July 4th. I recommended a pre-nup but Wes said he wanted to acquire her property, not the other way around. Her family owned a parcel from Oakland to Hayward that still is wild land. In the end, what're you going to do? It was his decision to marry, not ours."

"Did you come across any dirty dealing?"

"I looked for it, believe me. You investigate enough of this stuff, it eventually feels the same. That lady's father lost a chunk of change due to being outbid. Whatever they retained in the family is worth bucks. My superior Paul Litchstein reviewed my findings and he couldn't make it match."

"Were you aware another firm was brought in?"

"Yes. Josephine & Josephine out of Oakland. They produced more or less the same material. They felt Roark should make a codicil to his will which is what he finally had his attorney draw up."

"Did he at any time in your investigation give you the impression that he might not marry her?"

"Not once. He was taken with this woman. He got on well with her, they had similar interests, they knew some of the same people."

"Did he walk the line with any issues that could have caused him to become a target?"

"All these guys do. The over twenty million dollar per year millionaires all seem to think that playing with an expensive price tag can offset other difficulties they are encountering along the way. Roark went after Doppler radar which I think frankly is too single issue driven, then branched into privatization."

"Of water?"

"Yes. Can you imagine how many senators and farmers probably wanted to snare him over that one thing? The state certainly doesn't want to see loss of control over water rights."

❖ ❖ ❖

"There's no mention of it anywhere," Lina said, as she snacked on pecan rolls between portions of french toast and bacon at three in the afternoon. "What information did he send you?"

I consulted the slip. "Apparently Wes briefly entered computer farming for planting; but he seems to have developed the opinion that actual ownership of cropland should be discouraged. He also took over Doppler and then relatively quickly — a few months — exited it. It appears he was most comfortable among hard currency."

"He must've done quite well with stones."

"He probably did. He was sufficiently exploring the idea of improved security."

She said, "It's not hard to imagine. But his problem was of periodic, not continual, interference and thus was hard to find. This screen he used to produce photographs of actual scenes was infiltrated on an unpredictable basis by a prankster who infrequently altered his system. His museum was broken into, the timed release system for his commercial bank was altered thereby not giving him the access he required and the million ransom was stolen."

"Roark thought he knew what he was up against. He asked his assistant to deliver the ransom while he allegedly rode through traffic, then he abandoned his vehicle and somehow returned home, thereby avoiding the hotel scene."

"That's true."

"He had everyone out of the house at the time. His wife was talking to their solicitor, his son was working, his house staff all accounted for with various duties, leaving his chauffeur and assistant to handle the item."

"And then his son moved out."

"Didn't he eliminate Randall's access?"

"My guess is," I said thinking aloud, "that was why Randall

attempted access on Hauptman's system."

"No, that was too long ago."

"Just training?"

"Well, he was fourteen or fifteen." Then: "I can't help but wonder who brought Hart in."

"We know she was earning a livelihood as a landscape gardener in the neighborhood. It's probably how she met Randall."

"Makes you think someone fingered him first."

"Yes, it does."

"So, my question is who is the buyer and what did they want? Can we assume they got what they came for and that's why Roark is now dead?"

CHAPTER 15.

I STOOD IN TERRY'S FOYER.

She wiped tears that welled inside her eyes. "Randall is still on the run."

"Don't worry. Once the other side moves on the case, he'll return. He won't stay out there forever. He may be headstrong but Wes was his father. Without a father he'll feel the pangs of loss more sharply."

"I am without a past."

"He more so than you."

"Do you think he'll feel guilt?"

"He won't want to, but yes, I think it's somewhat inevitable."

"It's such a mess, all these loose ends."

"I'm sorry to have to leave."

"No, it's quite alright. Really. My mother's flying in. She's arriving tomorrow. I'll be fine."

"Have you thought about a funeral service? I'd like to come back if you're going to do one."

"Mr. Reese advised me not to have a public funeral. He said I'd attract less attention."

"Be well, and call if you need me."

She kept a stiff expression. "Thank you so much for everything," grasping my hands in hers. We stood quietly for a moment, then she released me saying, "Albert will be home soon."

"Take care," I said, and left.

CHAPTER **16.** LOS OSOS

I ATE BREAKFAST with Robert Brice and his new partner Francesca. Francesca was in her early fifties, a slender woman with wavy brown hair sculpted flat against an egg shaped head who wore bronze linen pants and matching jacket over a dark green sweater top and a dozen copper plated bracelets.

We kibitzed over bagels and lox and a spinach and tomato omelet about the Dow at the end of the trading hour and the NASDAQ dropping and about a plane that had spiralled into a building in a nose dive in the Fairfax district of Los Angeles. All evening Tammy Walt reported. A Sky 9 pilot had crashed ten minutes after take-off. The NTSB and FAA were at the scene. A sound of a stall spin had been detected and there was conjecture whether the turn had been too steep. Robert said it would have been impossible to recover from a turn so low to the ground. After five cups of coffee and an hour Robert paid the tab and he and Francesca took off. Robert and Francesca were going up to Monterey with his son and her two school-age children for a jazz festival and then camping at the beach. In an hour I would push off to Ventura for a half day and overnight on the beach in a small cottage owned by John's family for some private time to unwind from the frenetic week in Oakland.

The weather had reached a high of seventy with a low sixty-one. The news was still focussed on the Bonanza crash. Investigators were now investigating it as a terrorist attack. Assistant Chief Ron Smith of Los Angeles Police Department had gone to inspect the damage at the corner of Melrose and Spaulding where the plane had crashed at 4:00pm killing a person and injuring ten.

Between tilled fields of wheat a river had almost flooded over. Cut grass composited into square bales stood packaged to be sold as grain feed. Green rows of lettuce on richly brown soil flickered by. It'd be another four hours before I arrived in Ventura. A Coldwell Banker, a foster freeze and Kalijahn Associates crowded onto a corner across from a high school. On the other side of the mountain were weeping willow and aspen and wheat followed by substantial fields of strawberries and tomatoes. Beside a Bethel Assembly stood a fenced-in lot of engines, generators and boosters, a slice of impoverished life squeezed in between farms and villages.

By the time I arrived at the cottage, it was after five. The sky possessed a striated look interrupted at the horizon by a tinfoil ocean and scintillating light. I turned on the fireplace, washed my face, unpacked, then poured myself a whiskey which I took onto a veranda overlooking an unmarked sandy beach. The property had been the nest egg of John's mother's first husband who left it to her after he took a post in Honduras.

Now, drink in hand, I thought John and I would retire here if the relationship worked out. My salary was a good sixty grand and in another ten years was expected to top at seventy-five. Although John owned a flat in Florence, if he sold it he might net two hundred fifty thousand which would give us what we needed.

My thoughts turned to Wes Roark, to his achievements and his life, cut short at sixty-seven. I thought about his son and wondered what on earth had gone wrong, where the thing had begun to go wrong, why he hadn't been able to nip it in the bud. It didn't make sense that with his domestic holdings, anyone could have penetrated his securities holdings, let alone his life. Yet someone had walked through the front door into his study and shot him.

I carefully perused my notes to find anything I had missed. I had separated the major events as follows: Randall's apartment and his young friend who had days earlier gone to ask

Wes for money, and Randall's subsequent flight from the area; the various computer break-ins to friends and patrons of the Roark Museum; the artist Averty who was commissioned by Wes's wife Genieve to design gardens with decorative aqueducts; demand occurring so soon after Randall's alleged demand note to his mother; and his father's death. Also there was the deed for the property of fifty thousand acres of forested land including the area once known as Brooklyn to Sally Ann Roark's grandfather who disinherited a family member after the individual committed crime.

The Roark property which would be shared by Sally Ann Roark and her niece Genieve was cut down from fifty thousand to two hundred acres which constituted what they now owned. If it had been swindled there was no evidence in Sally Ann's papers. That information would have to be researched by going through Alameda County records and through documents in archives. There was very little I could do except to take a weekend or two to look for Randall and once found ask him to explain what his involvement was.

"You want to come ID a body? We retrieved it from the beach, surfing accident most likely. Male, approximate age eighteen, nothing on him in the way of driver's license."

"You think it's the son?" I peered into darkness at the neon clock on the mantel. The time was ten thirty.

"Dirty blond shoulder length hair, medium height, thin. Expensive trousers, satin shirt."

The attire did not match Randall's but I'd make the drive. "I'll be up in an hour."

In the dark I threw together a top and pant suit and grabbed a coat. The air was misty, the ground was wet from a fresh rain.

The drive to UCLA's lab took the better part of an hour. After the viewing I'd grab a breakfast of salami and a hard-boiled egg. I eyed the ocean, its roiling wave action, a lineup of beachfront homes, thick drapes pulled down over windows facing the highway. When I finally pulled into the emergency ward parking lot I found an unexpected combustion of ambulances and gurneys in wait for the arrivals of a gunshot wound and a stabbing.

In the first operating room marked Room A, stainless steel sinks, a crash cart and boxes of cloth drapes and plastic surgeons gloves were lined against a far wall. The body lay on an exam table, face up. I eyed it, then relieved shook my head to the tech. "It's not him."

"Well, you better talk to the lady in the hallway, says she's his wife."

"Is she Jane Hart?"

"She said she was Jane Roark. She's in the hallway."

I stepped out of the room. The woman was young, probably in her twenties, herself thin, with the distinction of having too young an appearance for her age. She was not what I had expected — cosmopolitan, stockinged in a business pantsuit, all lines of beauty the look of Fifth Avenue. If anything, she was somewhat unadorned, without appearing plain; merely pretty with red brunette hair to the shoulders held back in a rubber band, dark green blouse with sleeves, black pants, heeled sandals, the sort of woman who doesn't have to try hard to fit in. "Jane Hart?"

"Yes." She rose from her chair, her expression straining with tension. "Is he — dead?"

"Don't worry. It's not him," and I steered her further into the hall to a coffee vending machine. "Black?"

"No, cream and sugar, please."

"May I ask how you got here?" I popped a few quarters into the machine and pushed the button for cream and sugar. I handed her the cup.

She took it with shaking hands. "I returned to the beach house and was told Randall was taken in for concussion after he went under while surfing."

I popped another seventy-five cents in the machine for coffee and selected black. "Where were you staying?"

"At the home of a mutual friend."

"Do you mind telling me where?"

"It's in Morro Bay overlooking the beach. Are you familiar with it?"

"I know the area. Who said it was Randall?"

"A friend. A woman I've known for years."

"That wouldn't be Klee, would it?"

"No, I went roller blading and when I came back the police were there and Randall was gone."

"Did you get the name of the officer?"

"No, I was too much in a state of shock. I was driven here by a stranger."

"Is that person here now?"

"No. Are you sure it isn't Randall?"

"Positive."

"Because I wasn't allowed in. They said they were sending for someone who knew the family well. I guess that was you."

Her story didn't hold together, but it was her story and I had nothing with which to confront her on. I suggested we drive to her friend's beach house to see whether Randall might have returned. She was okay with the idea but wanted to get a look at the body.

"They won't let you because you're not a relation to the deceased," I said.

"I just thought I'd see what the man was talking about, why he thought it could be Randall."

"I'm sorry," I said, and nudged her gently to persuade her to come with me. "When did you last see him surfing?"

"Several hours ago. We went out together. Randall has more stamina than I do. I guess I might as well tell you. He's eight years younger than I am, and he can stay in the water all day."

I puzzled over this information. "Didn't you tell his father you were twenty-three years old?"

"His father told you about that? About my going to see him with the baby?"

"Yes, he was concerned about your intentions."

"Well, I'm serious about Randall, if that's what you mean. We had a child together."

"But you're older than he is. He's still a teenager in most respects."

"That's just age. He'll be eighteen in three months and then he can do anything he wants."

"But the family attorney said that he doesn't inherit until he's age twenty-five."

"I didn't mean it that way."

"What will you live on?"

"My wages and his trust. He told me all about it, how he's on a shoestring budget for the first seven years at eight hundred a month. It's okay. We'll survive."

"You garden?"

"From time to time. I can get a job anywhere. I type sixty words a minute and have worked for lawyers, doctors, computer firms, insurance agencies, stockbrokers. Just hire me and plug me in."

"That's an impressive resume."

We had reached my vehicle. I opened the door for her. From a profile I could see she was aging quickly, her jaw had a certain amount of slack to it, her neck skin pulled at her chin. I shut her door, then went around to the other side and slid in. I backed the car out of the lot and proceeded with caution around a stationary ambulance.

"Looks like it's been a busy morning," I said.

"Mmmm," she agreed. "It's true I met Randall because I was a gardener near the Roark's but I'd already run into Randall a number of times that year."

She'd dig her grave if she kept talking.

She continued with, "We met first at the Marketplace on

College Avenue. I had a job behind a counter at a chocolate fondue bar working for a friend. Randall came there with a girl. I overheard them talking and couldn't help remarking that I knew Roark in Sausalito."

"Do you know Genieve Roark then?"

"I know who she is. I've never met her."

"She's now Randall's stepmother."

"No, I've never met her."

"Not even when you went to see Randall's father?"

"No. Never."

"You have to admit the coincidence is rather striking."

"You make it sound as though I manipulated my meeting Randall."

"It's unusual for a teenager these days to wind up with an older woman."

"Randall and I have an honest relationship. Everything is spelled out."

"Do you mind my asking why you didn't encourage him to visit his father more?"

"Randall didn't want to. He said his father always expects things from him. You know, Ms. — "

"The last name is Cliford."

"Ms. Cliford. Randall is much more grown up than many guys my own age. Plus he's a whizz on the computer. He can do anything."

"I can appreciate that. By the way, what happened to his job for the professor at Ames?"

"That was just for six weeks to tie us over. When we had enough money, we drove down here."

"Morro Bay costs money. Even when Randall's trust becomes fully operable in another month, thirty-five hundred bucks isn't going to take you far."

"We'll make out."

We passed barren low lying hills. Irrigated and tilled fields of yellow and green cut the landscape into squares intersected only by railroad tracks. "Where are you from originally?" I asked her.

"Long Island. My family raised me in the suburbs where I met my first husband. His name was Bob. He had a daughter by a first wife. He was half East-Indian and he was a computer analyst working for a restaurant in Atlantic City in Jersey. He used to have me look over the programs, make sure any kid fresh out of school could operate what he came up with."

"What brought you to the West coast?"

"We came out one summer to talk to some guy who wanted Bob to baby-sit his warehouse. Well, it turns out this guy has a place in San Pablo on the water. Very funky, way back off the freeway, one stop past the race track at Golden Gate Fields."

"Out near Pt. Richmond?"

"Right. At Pt. Molate. So we board up on this guy's houseboat, very nice place, two story floater, and we have total run of the place. The guy takes us to San Mateo, introduces us to some very upscale people. That's how I met the Hauptmans, or the son at any rate. He was a talker. He had an angle. His father had this super big fish on the line and was going to reel him in on a line he came up with all by himself and take a closeup of one particular program."

"And did he?"

"I don't know whether anyone knows. Next thing he's dead. Or drunk and dead. His father's in New York for some hoopla and the cops have to call him with the bad news. I just split. I figured, what on earth do I need all this crap for, I'm not looking for trouble, so I ditched that scene. Next thing I know I'd run into Randall again. We just hit it off. You know how that is."

"Does the guy who introduced you to Hauptman have a name?"

She'd backed herself into a corner. "He's dead. He doesn't exist anymore. Nice man, but with one too many problems."

"Are we talking about Neil Holyer?"

"That's the last name. I'd forgotten it."

"What was his problem exactly?"

"I believe he tried to undercut the person who owned the warehouse."

"How did he do that?"

"He arranged for someone else to transport the goods to another location."

"What were the goods?"

"Art, I think."

"Could they have been museum artifacts?"

"Not likely. He was a surgeon."

"A trauma surgeon?"

"No, an internist."

She was definite, but I now had a larger picture of something I had not previously considered. "Did you ever meet a man named Hamilton?"

"No."

She pointed which exit to take. I exited on Freedom and headed toward the beach. The four or five acres of beach homes overlooking the shell rock and the three stacks that made up Morro Bay were the only sign of prosperity on this side of the hill. Four streets overlooked soft unblemished beach. She gave me the address and I zipped up the road to a nice glass affair which from the living room took in a million dollar view.

The man who answered the door and promised to have access to the owner had no idea where Randall had stumbled off to. Neither was Jane Hart's child present. A quiet fire burned on logs in an insert in the fireplace.

"Care for a beer?" Jane asked.

"Sure," I said, and took a seat on the sofa. "Where's your son?"

"A friend of mine has him."

"Is this friend nearby?"

Jane took two beer bottles from the refrigerator, uncapped them and gave me one. "You're awfully inquisitive."

"That's my job."

She shrugged. "Mick used to attend Santa Barbara," she said, motioning to the man who had answered the door.

Mick was busy welding metal together to make a choker. "You from the area?" He asked me.

"Alameda."

"Oh yeah, the kid's making a beeline for L.A. Aced himself another programming score. Big Money."

"Computers?"

"Yeah, he roped Janey and the Gov into it."

"Who's the Gov?" I asked her.

"He's my father's friend. Whenever I'm out of work he fixes me up with a little something."

"So you an artist, Mick?"

"As you see. I sell at craft fairs, the Salinas Artichoke Fair, handful of them. Plus I've got a gallery in Carmel and another I share with a handful of jokers in Monterey at Fisherman's Wharf. I make out okay. A hundred grand a year."

"Better than me."

"Well, a cop's pay can't be all that great."

"I'm a detective."

"Really? Ex cop?"

"Investigator for the courts and prison system out of Oakland."

"Yeah, you're a ways away from there."

"I took a weekend off but was called to ID what they suspected was Randall Roark's body. Turned out it was the wrong man."

"Janey thought it was Randall, 'cause he's been talking for awhile now about splitting. He got a call from his mom I guess. I don't know. He's moody, that one. Is he really only seventeen?"

"Yes," I replied.

"Jesus, I'm thirty. I feel old."

"Wait until you get to be forty-eight."

"That's you?"

"Yes."

"Well, I guess it has to happen sooner or later," to which we laughed. Mick added, "We heard Randall's old man was killed."

"Two days ago. He was shot."

"Criminee. I thought that's why he took off."

"He did this yesterday?"

"Went surfboarding according to Janey. I wouldn't have let him if I'd been here. Shock does mighty strange stuff to a person."

"He have any other friends in the area?"

"I wouldn't know." He looked at Jane. "Who was that bloke we saw him with that day in Ventura?"

She shook her head.

"We'd gone to Rialto to see a friend of Jane's and on the way back we stopped to dinner and this guy comes over to talk to Randall. Nice looking chap. Tall, red hair, chappy."

"How was he dressed?"

"Trousers, cotton shirt, long sleeved. High style. Bloke."

"Friend of the family?"

"Could've been. Randall calls him Reimer."

"Age?"

"Oh your age, definitely. He said he had an office at the Trident Group at Jacks Peak."

Jane sat still, cautious. I smiled at her reassuringly.

"A businessman?" I inquired.

"Reimer? Maybe his name is Reigis or Reiger?" Mick wondered.

"Weed," Janey tossed out, back in the conversation without discomfort, causing me to question what had happened to ease her off the mark.

"Not Weed. Might be Reider, no Reimer? Does that sound about right?"

"Could be," she replied, with facile attention. "The name's

on the marquis. You could drive up to see."

"Which marquis would this be?"

"In Monterey," Mick said. "Behind the Hyatt. Out near the airport, near California State Parks."

I said, "What would he have done for Randall down here?"

"He found Randall that job."

"You've got quite a memory," she told him, admiration in her tone.

"I can remember almost anything except where Randall was headed."

They twittered. I had the feeling I was getting in their way.

"I've got to push off," I said, and stood. "If Randall comes in, will you let him know I was here?" I scribbled my cell phone on the back side of my business card.

Wind whipped the air.

Mick had blundered into the unspeakable and Jane had barely tolerated it. Between them, psychoanalytic disorders took precedence shutting me out as the identified intruder.

Back in my car I plugged my laptop into the lighter and consulted the suggested map search. Yahoo, usually barely competent at producing accurate directions, spit out Jacks Peak. Monterey. It spit out Monhollan Road off Olmstead.

I deliberated how much driving I was up for. Young Randall had taken off for the moment, probably south toward the metropolis of L.A. Instinct told me Randall wasn't coming back, but where he had gone and for what reason were sheer guesswork. I had some ideas that the young heir was gearing up for a major piece of action, but action to a computer buff who had spent his last six weeks learning a database for Ames could be anything.

I wasn't sold on Jane Hart. She was too sophisticated for

a teen drop-out. Despite the impression I had of her as hanging out rent-free until her big role in the movies turned up, I thought she was indeed a gold digger hanging around until the two, or however many of them there were, could seize Roark's estate.

I called Trident and asked for Mr. Reimer. A secretary said the name was Weed and that he was out and would not be returning until morning. I then called Sylvan Reese, Roark's attorney, on the off chance the solicitor might know who Weed was and was told he was away on business. I left my name.

A left on Olmstead leads past a small airport lot and winds around on Fred Kane Drive to the terminal, airstrip and Million Air hangar. Today two United Express airplanes, colored silvery blue, stood in the hangar. I eyed the half dozen foot traffic entering and leaving the airport and made a loop to the first intersecting road, Garden Drive. The Infinity Group stood at 2600 Garden. Across the road were the three office buildings that comprised the Trident Executive Center.

I entered and paused in front of the marquis. The Brandeis Montgomery Group had three offices on the first floor; upstairs was Salinas Security and Malpaso Sonar which I figured was a communications firm of some type. I made a U-ie out of the lot and drove down to the golf course where two large tan blocks, one called the Salinas Room and the other the Monterey Room, stood facing the green. I returned the way I had come, this time passing the California State Parks and a security firm. A look-see at the marquis failed to produce the Weed banner, so I shot across the intersection leaving behind the airport drive and white taxi cab sitting like a beached young whale on the shoulder and drove up Monhollan Road.

A Foothill School sign advertised "smoking prohibited on campus" and contained a circular drive for five buses. Next to it opposite the road sign Via Malpaso sat a small office building with glass windows and a long courtyard evident from the road. The name Weed & Marsden appeared in copper letters on a grey nameplate nailed into a massive grey rock which fronted a patio with benches. I parked and went inside the courtyard. It was typical New Orleans French Quarter with a fountain made of nymphs in various stages of undress, their ridiculously thin arms supporting a smaller pool, the larger pool beneath their feet laden with quarters and nickels.

I passed inside to a dark corridor that led to an office. The walls were ensconced in scarlet swirls of velvet, blood red thick drapes over tall ceiling to floor windows, the floor a rich mahogany. The man at the desk glanced at me with utmost deference. He was a thin french man with a pastiche of moustache, his hair a pate. Grey eyes which could have been wistful weren't, him having succumbed to some sort of age of reason. A pseudo entrance to another office looking much like a crypt was painted in dark faux. French doors opened onto a small wrought iron balcony taking in the dark forest of Jack's Peak.

"You Weed?" I asked, as I eyed gilded framed oil paintings of scenes of the American Revolution, a gas lamp and a marble bust of Abraham Lincoln.

"I am. And you are?"

"Lenny Cliford," I answered, and gave the man my card. "I understand you found Randall Roark a job."

Weed appeared startled. "I encountered him a week or so ago, but it was an accidental meeting. He was in town in Los Osos with Janey whom I've known for quite some time. Do you know Jane Hart?"

"I've just come from visiting her. Is she a longtime acquaintance of yours?"

"We used to spend Saturdays together going grocery shopping or to the fish market in Carmel."

"This was before she met Randall?"

"Yes. He would've been twelve or thirteen."

"How did you meet her?"

"I once had a job at the Oakland estuary cleaning cages when she came along to feed the ducks. She was very youthful, perhaps twenty-two, although not yet completed in her studies at Laney Jr. College. She was tall, sturdy, wore long stockings, tap shoes, crimson skirts, velvet black tops, velvet scarves and hats. Fashionable. Nice." He smiled displaying a lopsided smile of teeth.

"She was a gardener."

"That was later."

"After the Hauptman suicide?"

"Oh, that was no suicide. Knowles was depressed but he had wealth. He wasn't on a jag, if you know what I mean. He intended to someday purchase a movie set of furniture — you know, Geddes, Fischer, the real stuff."

"How was it Janey entered that life?"

"Other way around. We were hobnobbing with the rich and we fell into the acquisitions set — those whose families were old money with deeds. Janey thought we should open a shop, I thought we should sell privileged art for customers the likes of which Neil Holyer felt would use our talents for life, a sort of captive audience."

"So Neil brought you in?"

"Oh, no, man. He merely shopped for Mr. Roark; he didn't staff for those sort of families unless he knew them personally."

"Did he bring young Roark into the fray?"

"No, that would've been Hauptman — or Jones, who was notorious for educating the young set in all sorts of wicked things, drinking, marijuana, gambling, box car racing and databases." He added, laughing at his own joke.

"Jones claims he offered the boy a summer job and that whatever career he found himself in was happenstance. That's Jones. He shrugs most things off. Very noncommittal chap. Please, have a seat."

I sat on an adjacent armchair upholstered in black satin.

"The night Hauptman's son died — "

"What about it?"

"Were you in Sausalito?"

"I was in New York with Hauptman at his opening."

"And Janey? Where was she?"

"Not here either as far as I know. Young Hauptman had too much to drink, stumbled blind into the garden and must have tripped and fallen on a rock surface into the pool. He drowned."

"Did you know Sally Ann Roark?"

"Yes, yes, I knew all of them. Wes, Adam, Gen — "

"You know Genieve Roark?"

"She's a Canber. She was very close to Knowles."

"So you met Janey. Who introduced her to Randall Roark?"

"She introduced herself."

"Not one of Roark's business associates? Like yourself?"

"It wasn't me. She had landed a job in the Piedmont through a service and had seen him drive by in a Packard convertible. Naturally she gravitated to him."

It was a long distance to fall from gardening an upper class estate to bringing the heir's son to collect on a presumption from his father and then to wind up in a box house on a hillside in Morro Bay. Something, some idea, some notion had to have attracted her to him to have lugged him around like misplaced suitcases.

"Any racketeering in her family?" I asked him.

"Not to my knowledge."

"What does one need to know to look for to know one is dealing with a crime ring? Large bank deposits with no visible method of income?"

"None." He smiled stiffly, unamused, interest beginning to wane.

"Randall had some high resolution, ready camera weave patterns on it and it made me think of currency. It struck me that he might be testing color of background for counterfeit bills."

"You have an overactive imagination. May I suggest another idea?" He asked and launched into it. "Randall's father specialized in color ink. Of course the mere concept of color causes one to think immediately of currency, but don't you think it is possible the man speculated in art forms of all types?"

"For example?"

"Well, certainly you can see where we are going with this. He has silhouettes, then he has graphics and shadow boxing, then actual drawings and water color, photographs of the scenes from which the drawings are made, wooden and plastic moulds, and lastly miniature cement structures. All these are used on his databases. If you penetrate these, you penetrate his system."

"I see you've given this some thought."

"Well," Weed feigned modesty, "the facts of this man's acquisitions are inescapable. Any art he purchases eventually is used as a focus for decoupage for a security system."

"Sort of like for an orientation into a database?"

"Precisely. The delicate weave for background is itself useful and if it matches whatever item is on the screen when the timed releases are moving into place, then viola! One can actually take a fax photo and substitute a portion of it for that similar portion of the screen saver. In the time it takes another camera to identify the fraud, the locks can be opened and the theft can have occurred."

"Do you know what type of security system Mr. Roark had for his various institutions?"

"Yes. These are complex systems. The locks are timed released and the computer program is reset usually weekly. With an unusual screen saver catalogue file, it is virtually impossible to penetrate."

"Unless the entire system is closely monitored by outsiders."

He conceded with a look that struck me as guilty knowledge.

"Do you know who might be interested in hiring people for this?"

"The most obvious answer is a buyer for the pieces Roark has on display for which the recovery fee would be exorbitant."

"Such as his farmland sketches."

"There are those. First and foremost there is the Berlin diamond. Then there are his Dutch pieces of light — his most noteworthy are the ruby colored translucent images — which have earned the Roark Museum its reputation.

"He acquired these perhaps fifteen years ago from a little known artist in Holland. The artist had an epiphanic style such that the square and diamond shapes revealed a series of deepening red quality. These canvasses were all mounted beneath lights which allowed them to appear as though they pulsated. From a distance these paintings seem like softly glowing orbs in an underwater, dreamy landscape."

"Did Neil Holyer put the show together?"

"I believe it was Terry, his first wife, although I couldn't be certain."

"Do you know whether Jane Hart ever saw this exhibit?"

"Yes, she did. Numerous times."

A cool strobe light emanated from the Morro Bay home. Discordant, somewhat clashing jazz sounds bleated in a lost anxiety through an open window.

Jane led me into the dimly lit living room. The view was of inky darkness as warm and as fluid as the stillness of the rocky harbor and its PG&E stacks. Jane wore black tights and a heavy white terricloth robe draped around her shoulders. Her hair down, makeup gone, she looked Randall's age, although I knew the hard certainty of her voice would cancel the impression.

"Did you ever see the ruby red abstract paintings at the Roark Museum?" I inquired.

"The red zone?"

"Vera showed them to her," Mick's voice inserted itself into the ambiance, "while they were still in boxes at the warehouse in downtown Oakland."

Jane looked sleepily for him and seeing him reached for his hand, not noticing her bathrobe open to reveal pendulum breasts resting securely on a thin rib cage.

"Who is Vera?" I asked, averting my gaze to Mick.

He took Jane's hand in a confession of tenderness. "Vera was Randall's black market contact," he replied. In his state he was naked although he was dressed in white cotton lounge pants and a matching top. "Vera Dermott. She should be in the white pages."

"For which city?"

"Piedmont."

"Why would Randall want a black market contact?"

"She brought in people to do imitative art."

"Why not sell prints of an original?"

They gave me smiles that said I was naive. Mick said, "Well, for one thing the original's going to run a good thirty-five to forty thousand dollars at a minimum."

"More if the market will bear it," Jane interjected.

"Most art collectors want the real item."

"Is Vera also a fence?"

"You should talk to Randall. She stores the items until the price hits above say thirty grand and then releases them only by arrangement."

"Do you know whether she has any in storage now?"

Mick deferred to her, but Jane had raised her guard. "Randall'll be back in a few days. Why not ask him then?"

I didn't want to wait. Chances were Randall had a job to pull and I didn't want to discover after the fact that I had let too much time lapse when I could have done something.

"Is there any possibility that that particular exhibit was chosen with the internal security system because it is dark with a depth that a camera might not readily pick out?"

Her face hardened. "I heard Randall say his father brought in a team of experts to test it against his systems already in place."

"You mean like an infrared system?" Mick suggested.

"I'm not sure what I mean. I'm just thinking aloud."

"Randall tested the system on his own." Mick remarked.

"Did his father know that?"

Jane answered. "He had a row with him over it. Apparently at night the pictures resemble objects rather than flat surfaces. The diamond shapes on the floors become like large translucent rubies."

Mick gave a comprehending nod. "I see what you're getting at. You think he picked over his father's system."

"Sort of sounds that way, don't you think?"

"Maybe Randall's old man should've kept the mounts on walls as he did to begin with."

"Any idea why he changed?"

"It was the recommendation of his security. Man by the name of Shotwell down in Salinas Valley. My guess is the pictures look very different when seen as a corridor of glass."

"He took a job for one of the Bolivars," Robert Shotwell said about Randall.

Shotwell had started as an artist of some repute known for his mixed media. Following several successes he put together security for light show artists, blending entrance shots with camera capture so that as an unsuspecting public entered the room they proceeded down a tunnel of angles into the main event, cameras taking breath captivating photographs of close-up and profile shots.

"Any idea as to how young Randall might have done this?"

"He did it with a series created by Mitchel Hauptman."

"The ruby corridor?"

"Well, Randall, I understand, tried to infect the security to create a release such as the opening of a door to bypass an alarm. We all thought he intended to do a job on his father's museum. Simple in principle, but then that's Randall. He likes fooling around with doors and windows to figure out where a person inside a building could get lost."

"Is that how the Bolivars pulled off the heist of the Rose Bowl stadium?"

"I think their most recent job was the Sante Fe stadium in the desert which not only resembles a train station but has a similar layout to a stage coach, if you will, of telegraph offices nationwide. Of course the architect no doubt envisioned this for the popular appeal to county residents who until recently were largely retired railroad employees, but for those few who would be jewel thieves this is no easy in, easy out."

"But the Bolivars walked off with what was it? A game's take?"

"Roughly. They staged a diversion that had a cops and robber chase while simultaneously a cashier operating from a van transferred the deposit from the stadium bank to an offshore location."

"Maybe the money never left the area."

"Could be. I wouldn't know."

I looked up Klee before I left the area. Her name was listed in Los Osos at a motel. I drove the ten or so miles to the shabby Motel 6 and knocked on her door.

The woman who opened the door was as used up as the weather-beaten overnight rat trap she was living in.

"Mrs. Klee?"

"Yes?"

"Investigator Cliford. I understand your husband is still at large. May I come in?"

"You can't come in here. It's a mess." She stepped outside in bare feet. She was her daughter, once pretty and youthful, exuberance sapped out of her. She wore her long curly black hair in a pony tail.

"Any idea what he's up to?"

"Robbing the Lourve or hanging by a rope."

"I beg your pardon?"

"He started his career in hotels, lowering a rope through glass into the state room and robbing the safe. He does it now for the exercise."

I smiled. She'd be a comedienne someday.

"Do you know a woman named Jane Hart?"

"Tell her to go to hell. She wanted me to strap on a cable and dangle through a skylight into a bank and pull a job."

"Did she say which bank?"

"No, and I didn't ask."

"You did a good job with your daughter. She's a nice girl."

She scoffed. "She'll wind up his carbon copy or worse. He started in ballet too."

"Where?"

"In London. On the second story of a studio a block from a train station."

In her business there was always an angle. It was probably the one thing that kept her dangling from a rope for her adult life.

CHAPTER 17.

THERE WAS MONEY to be made.

I toyed with a wooden toy horse painted pink and white as I waited for Adam King's response. He wore linen pants, a tweed polo over a stiff collared white shirt, a plain jacket and smart yellow loafers. We sat in Adam's dining room in his thatched roof cottage in Diamond Canyon above the golf course. Fully recovered from his ordeal he was his old self, a congenial consultant in his mid sixties who although paid for his expert knowledge about European stocks had been nevertheless retained for his ability to spot trouble long before it materialized.

At length he acknowledged the obvious. "Randall wanted a windfall. He idled on the pool patio, supped with this Hart woman, ate his father out of house and home and in his absence apparently held parties for her friends, attracting a dubious sort onto the premises for God knows what. When Wes confronted Randall on it, Randall moved out. He was not to be reasoned with, let alone governed by whatever it is that chills a mad hen."

"I suppose parents try a tough love approach."

"If it works. Wes was reticent to do this. He had had one too many run ins and had backed down assuming as many of his friends did that if he could ride out his son's rebellion he would be able to salvage their relationship in the long run."

"What did Randall want?"

"His own vehicle, bank account, password to his father's museum. Finally he got it by trickery of some sort. He had over-committed on a deal and was in an embarrassing situation in which he had to produce on what was essentially his father's signature. I offered to research the questionable authenticity but Wes said absolutely not."

"Any possibility you could do that now?"

"Since Wes was killed, the FBI have frozen all accounts. I wouldn't be able to enter those databanks without setting off warnings in all directions."

"Do you know which accounts?"

"Security related. Metal doors, laser, alarms, satellite enhancement, coding and then something he referred to as zero bases."

"What do you mean by zero bases?"

"Systems of databases — Tiffany and Harbord. There's sixty basic systems and then groupings of variations. Wes put together situations which were comprised of fairly complex systems."

"With this high level security wouldn't it be a simple matter to infiltrate if you could interface with names of systems?"

"It's done. That's why Wes used drawings to offset the likelihood of infiltration."

"Was he interested in what Randall was up to?"

He said, "You betcha. Wes worked his son's system with a fine tooth comb. The obstacle course of ruby objects is virtually impenetrable because the stone it was designed to protect is a bluish diamond. It cannot be detected in the dark because of the ruby corridor. The agent was experienced with Tiffany, which is your most elaborate system because it works with timed release light.

"If in typing in your command, you can't get into your system and you can't open any programmed door, if when your security off-site punches in a bailout code to penetrate the key pad with high frequency sound, if you lose Bell capability, you can enter the computer which monitors your system."

"How many times did Wes experience difficulties?"

"Daily for one period lasting four hours."

"Was that length of time significant?"

"Very much so. In general it would have been anyways. The typical infiltration device was the number 4 which shaped like an H, when turned over on its side, becomes a prong. When inserted on the page your hacker can lift the entire page off the screen. 4H is used for hieroglyphics."

"If he thought a problem was internal, what would he do?"

"He would terminate a company, possibly by filing a chapter 11 or 13, and open a new business in another city to reduce the continued risk of infiltration."

"So potentially his son could seriously affect his registrar."

"Yes. But it didn't happen to that extent. The worst problem was that his vaults were tampered with."

"Which suggests what?"

"Could be anything. Use for theft, stadium or concert, or vandalism to his museum."

"Did Wes consider these possibilities?"

"Thoroughly."

"Any thoughts as to who shot him?"

"It's unlikely it was his wife even though she had access. I'd look for a skillful interloper."

Or someone who knew the layout of the first floor. Someone like Jane Hart.

Chapter 18.

"THE HEART, YOU SAY?"

The speaker was Henry Hargrave Bolivar, cousin to the two brothers whose notorious feats brought them their reputation as managing crooks of stadium and concert heists. Like other family members he was tall, tan in his face and arms, rounded head, relatively flat features, a flap of straight brown hair over a lined forehead, large dark eyes and nondescript mouth. A bookkeeper by trade, he was today a furniture salesman whose store across the street from the Radison Hotel saw tourists and politicians alike whose business interests could be deduced from the company they kept.

I had found Henry Hargrave as a result of a thorough database search for surveillance systems in San Bernardino which matched high tech, high profile users of art systems anywhere in the state. Henry sold Deskey, Geddes, and a handful of other venues from the fifties. Because he outfitted sleazy dens, lower East side type restaurants, college bars and the like, his name appeared frequently in local jazz and arts magazines.

"Jane Hart had a son who as I understand it resembled Roark in the face and upper body. He was an artist living in Marin around the time Bert Hauptman died, and Hart disappeared shortly thereafter. It's anyone's guess what she wants with Roark but I'd start there. If he had lived he'd be in his late twenties."

"You must mean a brother. She's in her late twenties."

"Not the Jane Hart I knew. Try early forties."

"You have a name for him?"

"Laddie," he said, and chortled causing his face to darken even more.

I smiled politely.

"I wouldn't have known, to be honest. If she wants my

cousin to take a look-see at young Roark, it's for a reason. It wouldn't be something I'd do."

"Maybe Hart was last seen in the Bern before he disappeared."

"I sell furniture. If I have to, I run up to Seattle and take several days to Trojan Park and the coast to pick up estate pieces rusting in someone's backyard. I always offer to take my cousins with me if their parents are snowed in."

I couldn't tell where Henry was going with this. "Did you offer to take Hart?"

"Well, if a young artist is down on his luck, sooner or later if they're to be taken in and looked after, they head up for those parts. Once there, they'll stick him in the saddle right away. Or he'll wind up with a woman like Hart who'll take him in and give him free run of the house."

"Perfect setup for a young man like Randall Roark."

"No kidding. Bel Geddes be damned, eventually half of the Bern's kids take off for Trojan Park. If he hasn't thought of it yet, if he actually does hook up with my cousin, he'll be on the first Princess line north as kitchen help."

"Getting back to Jane — "

"Sure."

"Who was she married to?"

"Oh, Hart's her maiden name I'm pretty sure, and I doubt she was ever married for long. No, no, I see why you're asking. Who's the father of her son? Damned if I know. I will say that for a brief time she knew this guy up in Martinez near the Veterans Hospital and he pretty much stole the show. Glitzy kind of guy. Good looking, dark wavy hair, tall, thin, mustache, drove a sportscar. Someone would probably remember him."

"Makes you wonder why she gravitated to young Roark at all, if it was just his looks."

"The computer stuff. Remember she's the going concern in a world of upwardly mobile professionals and rising upper class. These folks have hit pay dirt. They're born out of immigrant farmers and shoes salesmen and they've entered the ranks of our senate and assembly, of our stockbrokerage houses, they're yacht owners, merchants, restauranteers, you know the profile. Children of the fifties. It's a period thing."

I knew. Life was only best if there was easy coin to ditch into the cruise ship casino, take a spin at Roulette or take cocktails in the Gold Rush paddle room. For the few who invested wrong and set their sights too high at the racetrack, the descent to hell came at a steep price, and an even steeper fall.

Jane Hart had the experience of a fully ripened woman, one who in addition to knowing her mind also could when needed select targets or subjects, hone in on them and put them to sleep and wake them up. It was two years since she identified the Roark residence and decided to use Randall, if only to force Wes to retreat from subjects of inquiry or from investments. By creating an avenue of disclosure, she would open the templates for enhanced databases and if she were lucky she might succeed in learning where entries were stored. If this was a system she knew something about, the implication was she was looking to learn where the stinger was.

Retrievable information sites were not the simplicity they appeared to be. Far from unlocking missiles and launching weapons of mass destruction, retrievable pins were combinations for safes, descending shields for unique art, critical captures on wall street, not to mention information he kept secured in underground vaults to penetrate areas of denied access. Hart's ability to stagger response times of seeing eyes, to close off programs without activating alarms made sense.

Wes' primary objective would be to find out who was tampering. Hart's objective was to turn off systems while also staging break-ins. Bank seizures, capital ventures were probably too visible, leaving wide trails in open charted territory. If she had helped the two Bolivars to empty a banking transfer made at the Sante Fe stadium after a baseball game to an undisclosed, never-to-be-identified account, then it had been accomplished because it had occurred once. Her focus today would be no different than in the past, if only for the reason she could not earn what she was accustomed to any other way. But in San Bernardino the possibilities to stab a tool bar into a well monied vein were limited. If she was not looking at a concert or box car event then it was some other cash turnip. The problem with going after a reservation casino was the store never put the doors where one could exit easily. Just as the complicated security system hid access, so did entries and exits. If one got in, one couldn't get out. Many a robber quickly discovered that the door they thought led to a parking lot actually led to the executive washroom and a pair of cufflinks.

Here she was in Los Osos. If she needed glasses she would pick them up here. Then it would be to Bolivar with possibly a stop at one of his contacts. If she were on a schedule, it stood to reason Randall was doctoring a system for later use.

A million in cash had been stolen. Adam King had nearly lost his life. Roark had been killed. A funeral had been discreetly done. The will had not yet been read. The distance from Roark's home to the end of the street block of his neighborhood was approximately the length of a Princess cruise liner. Since his death a patrol car sat at his estate and another at the end of the block. When the program governing his staff and house was changed and any problems corrected, it should become apparent why the group focussed on Roark's home rather than on the headquarters of his considerable holdings. Logic said Roark's bank was located somewhere between Los Osos and the Bern. Logic also said that after Roark, King and son were exited, the person with the most authority and control was Genieve Roark.

By the time I returned to the beach home Randall had left. A new face answered the door.

"Is Jane here?" I asked.

"You just missed them. They're traveling to the desert to

her home there."

"Where is it?"

"At one of the park entrances, I forget which, but you can't miss it. It's a large two story adobe house with a ladder to the second story window from a ledge."

"How does she afford to live there?"

"She does the news," he replied, and made it sound like noose. He indicated by wiggling the crook of his forefinger that she had a job writing captions.

"Thanks."

"Don't mention it."

The drive south took me through dense forests and rolling plantations crowded with stakes. In line with the stretched out horizon the asphalt grew thinner and the car lots and ranches and snack bars and high schools whipped by simulating a peculiar road test. Signs elbowed out Tudor hotels and stone castles. A carnival of people standing on a platform came and went and with them big splotches of water poured out of the sky making the road sticky dark. A window seen from its side in a pickup passed. The hills and shimmering aspen turned into rock with icy blue patinas and short grasses.

By the time I made it to Lina's home, it was nine o'clock. Lina and Max were finishing a late supper and were taking coffee and sherbert on the patio before an outdoor fireplace. I caught her up to date on my trip with the particulars about Jane Hart.

"It's probably a routine splash," Lina said, when I was done.

"Any way to find out?"

"You have a phone number for him?"

"Phone, address, birthdate and social security."

"With that I can do anything. I'll bring it to work."

"Great."

"I'd like to propose something here."

"Sure, what?"

"Randall's been at this a long time. He can detect a pass. His system will no doubt contain a way to tag us as I make an approach."

"Just a peek is all."

"Why not use a consultant, someone with capability to maneuver around detection."

"Do we have such a person?"

"Well, I do. His name is Frap."

"Who is he?"

"He does security for the stadium."

"Yes. Give me his number."

She handed me a card. On it was a picture of a faucet.

"Looks like Monopoly."

"I think it's what he does. When he collects a bin, he has a backup program which selects words for parallel processing against federal communications coding. If more than seven words have matches or can provide decoding for the alphabet, the subject is considered a hacker."

"Thanks. Can I call him now?"

"He is never closed to us."

Frap's file was thin. The two Bolivars were cited with a stadium drawer robbery and a series of drivebys in Rialto and the Bern. More than that was conjecture. There was some idea they created false passports, bought into the cruise line business and walked a line between love and death with a handful of cemeteries sprinkled throughout the desert. The older Bolivar had married an actress who was rumored to have murdered a son.

I telephoned Officer Ames in Oakland. He wasn't in. I talked to the on duty deputy, a man named Regular, and read him the file.

"The son didn't die," Louis Regular said. "He's an autistic in a nursing home. You see alot of this stuff when you're dealing with bag men."

"You have the name of the home?"

"Tri-City Sanitorium. It's in southern Fremont, almost to Santa Clara."

"How about a name?"

"Milton Cousins. His mother was the actress Gabriella Cousins."

"Never heard of her."

"She did a remake of Beauty and the Beast, of Finnegan's Wake, the Graywolf Expedition, and a handful of films for television. Tall, silver blonde, curly hair to her waist, hourglass figure, odd cheekbone structure."

"What was wrong with it?"

"Too many bones. A very talented actress."

"Was Milton her only son?"

"I think she had another but that's conjecture."

"Why do you suppose Bolivar had him committed?"

"The kid was a goner. He had an accident as a teenager that left him semi paralyzed with a cleft. The surgery fixed the cleft but left the jaw slightly out of kilter."

"That must've been tough sailing for Bolivar."

"Bolivar didn't care. I think he gave him up because he's little more than an imbecile. Maybe the accident ended the marriage. It's never clear cut with these types of situations."

"Any idea who knows the full story?"

"You might try the sanitorium owner, woman by the name of Vera Stranger."

"Funny name."

"Them and doctors. You get used to it. Names like Slaughter, Bruiser, Lucifer — sooner or later you get your fill of it. If you'd like, I'll dig the name out of the phonebook."

"That'd be terrific."

"Yeah, here it is." He rattled off the number. Then: "Best of luck. We'd love to be able to nail Bolivar."

"So would we. Tell Officer Ames I said hello."

I ran a clearance on Vera Stranger. She had a hit as a complainant in a harassment citation for an address in Oakland. Map Search put her on the other side of Mills College near the Mormon and Greek Temples.

Her property was a good two to three acres. Set off the road, the drive wended through tall grass and snarly oak trees, their thin trunks studded with green lichen, branches bare. The sky showed through as a bluish grey landscape capable of descending in an invisible sheet. As I retreated further and further leaving behind all sounds of the road and city, I felt the sting of the investigation dissipate and with it the impatience that crept back into my mood.

The house was made of yellow sandstone. Clear jeweled windows in the entry sparkled like crystal from a goblet. The door was grey. The suggestion of a deck appeared through a window and appeared to extend like a long diagonal to clustered oak trees.

The woman who answered was African American, medium height, slender, with shoulder length hair coiffed at the bottom. She wore a pearl knit white sweater with low collar and a black traditional knit skirt with slip on leather heels. She said she was Vera Stranger and stiffly invited me inside.

The entry and living room were dark wood floors with a built-in bookshelf just inside the large room. Two upholstered navy couches with matching throw pillows sat around a overly large fireplace made of somewhat unattractive large stones. Jeweled ceiling to floor windows opened onto a slate patio made of dark grey stone. We sat on opposite couches. Ms. Stranger offered me a mint out of a metal box meant for cigars. I declined politely.

"I am seeking information about a woman named Gabriella Bolivar," I said, and handed her a court document permitting disclosure of information.

She barely held it letting it slip through her fingers onto the couch. "Gab lives in Montclair near the Fire Department.

She comes weekly to visit her son. Sometimes she is brought by her friend Carole Price and sometimes she comes alone. She almost always stays the complete time allowed for visitation. She isn't late on the fee and doesn't skimp on incidentals."

"How did her son become crippled?"

"He is alleged to have been in an accident that almost took his life. When he came to me, he was in the condition you see him in today."

"Have any of the Bolivars visited him?"

"His father Eduard comes every so often. The last I saw him he came with his brother Yasman approximately a week ago to discuss moving him to a more private facility across town, one I also own. We agreed he would be transferred that weekend. However, when we attempted to move him, he came undone."

"What do you mean exactly?"

"He became gravely upset. He displayed twitching and bizarre arm movements. I took no chances. I cancelled the order and wheeled him back to his private room overlooking the magnolia garden. I had him sedated and placed a nurse to watch him twenty-four seven. I changed his diet, his bed, and had my nurse take vital signs every half hour. Then I attempted to contact Mr. Bolivar. I reached an answering service, was told he was under arrest and awaited his response which as a matter of fact did not come for two days."

"This would have been Yasman Bolivar?"

"Yes, I have no telephone for Eduard."

"What about for Gabriella?"

"She has no phone. Yasman is my sole contact for the family."

Now I understood a chain of events behind the scenes. One Bolivar was a broken man, the other was a shyster. Who the hell knew what event took him to the Hyatt Hotel at the exact time of the Roark ransom? For all anyone knew Yasman Bolivar had gone to his brother's room for a drink when he was yanked by the police.

"How long has Milton Cousins been in residence?"

"Twenty years. His admission date was on August 10, 1984."

"Do you have an address for Ms. Cousins?"

Gabriella Cousins was beautiful despite the weariness that seemed to slump her shoulders. She was tall, a silvery light blonde, tumbling curls to her waist, thin shoulders, large pendulum breasts beneath a dark red sweater, an even thinner bodice, thin through the hips and long legged in black stretch pants. Her eyes were blue, her complexion flawless, wrinkle free. A series of face lifts could have done no worse. Her voice though was the coarse vulgarity of the west Oakland streets. It held a slur of hurried, pressured speech resonant of hard times and devastating consequences. Her son, her marriage, whatever other secrets she clung to, they ate up her dignity, not to mention her lustre. She held herself together like a chump who'd seen too many cocktail hours and had wound up taking home the gin bottle with the wino.

"I had a good life once upon a time. I was young, in love, on stage and in every way adored. If I'd kept my head, not a fucking thing like what's struck me woulda happened. I'm not trash. I came from money. Jesus!" Deprecating laughter spilled out of her. "I had a nice life. I had my career, a guy who wined and dined me in sequins and furs. None of what happened woulda come this close if I hadn't screwed it up."

I thought I understood her need to unburden herself. As soon as she gave her life story, we could get down to the real tasks that could require insight. "What happened?" I asked, as she lit a cigarette.

She removed an ashtray made of light blue glass. "I let myself get conned is what and Eddie took it outa my hide. I begged him not to get so goddamn heated up. I'm not cheatin' on you, love, I tol' him. But I got needs. I gotta git out, see some action, not stay locked up in a room in th' middle of nowhere. He fuckin' beat me, broke my nose, put me in th' hospital. I was so bruised I couldn't touch my skin."

"How come you didn't press charges?" I asked.

"You don' git it, do you? Let me tell you about Eddie. He'd just as soon stick a knife in yer rib as give you some money to have a little fun with. Yas is worse. You do it your way and he cuts your face. Great guys, right? I fell fer another guy. I tol' Eddie, I said, babe, I didn' mean to leave, I jus' went home. I had a guy before I ran into Eddie. A sweet, sweet guy. He's the one who lined up the audition fer me." She began to cry.

I slipped a photograph of Randall Roark into her slightly open cupped hands. "Take a look, Gabriella. Do you know him?"

She lifted her glance. "Sure. I've met your client, Randall. He useta come see Milt with his friend."

"Who was his friend?"

"Hart," she said, with sudden venom. "That filthy bitch! She has more gall than you kin believe. She stood there and said I'd never leave that grown baby. I coulda slapped her but Randall wouldn't let me." She blinked back false tears. "Kin you imagine? She sashayed right inta the room. Smug."

"Why didn't you want her there? Did she cause the accident?"

"Eddie wanted me to keep her at my house before the accident, and I said, sure, babe, anything you want. Milt was in good shape then, worked out every day, came with me to hear Carole sing."

"But you and your husband were divorced?"

"Ed's not my husband. He was my stage manager."

"Is he Milt's father?"

"Step father. He sort of looked after things after Milt slipped."

"I thought he was in an automobile accident."

"Oh right. We were living across the bay then."

"Where?"

"In Belvedere."

"Did you know the Hauptmans?"

She nodded. "I was an item with Bert Hauptman."

"Behind his wife's back?"

She scoffed. "There wasn't much going on in that department."

"Did you know Geneva?"

"Sure. We all know Geneva."

I waited for the explanation.

"Geneva is the class act. She grabbed the Hauptman nightclub when she became a partner. She didn't need Bert, or want him," she said in her own defense. "She was on the make all the time."

"For whom?"

"Not for whom. For what. She gobbled up every pieca land she could get her hands on. The Soundless Wave. The parcel in Hayward, the one up near Pardee Dam. You can't hold her back, trust me. I wouldn'ta been involved if it weren't for Bert." Her voice cracked on his name.

I did the arithmetic. "I thought your son was at the sanitorium twenty years."

"It's been about that."

"How old is he?"

"Forty."

I was surprised. "How old are you?"

She smiled sublimely. "Ninety." She laughed raucously and shook her head in another moment of self criticism. "I'm seventy-nine," she amended her age.

"You look terrific."

"So everyone says. That's what acting gives you. Poise."

"Were you there when Bert fell?"

"No. That was the one time I wasn't with him. It's a weird coincidence, isn't it?"

It was too odd to be ignored. "Do you know who was inside the house?"

"Geneva was, trust me. Scheming her schemes. Ignoring Bert, letting him get so sloshed she couldn't git him off the patio inta the house."

"I spoke to Hans Hauptman — "

"What do you think he's going to say?!" She demanded. "He is in business with her. He's got a claim with her."

"They're in the restaurant business. Is that what you mean?" I knew it wasn't but found her idea of what the picture should be was blurred.

"Look at me. I useta be pretty." She retorted, as though my view misrepresented her idealism. "I useta be someone. I was in the flicks. I gotta right to be here. Milt's the same as me. He got me the audition. He drove me to the studio every day. We had a cottage right there on the set."

"Was this before or after Bert died?"

"After. Bert died in 1976 and soon after I started the re-lationship with Milt's father. I never felt so much love for one man in my life. You have to have a man. Without love one withers."

It was a moment for profound thoughts.

"Where is Milt Cousins today?" I asked.

"Eddie ran him outa town, tol' him not to come round no more. I liked to live. I liked my fun. Without my sweet, cute man — " Her voice cut up on her. "I couldn't get outa bed. I didn't wanta live. I tol' Eddie I'd do better next time. I said I'd do anything. All he had to do was ask."

She looked imploringly at me, a washed up beauty star whose life was encapsulated in a chunk of memories.

I said, "Where is Milt's father? Perhaps I could try to locate him for you."

"It can't be done. He's as gone as he'll ever be. I jus' gotta get useta that fact."

"I'm sorry."

"No one's sorrier than me."

"Any ideas about Randall? I know for a fact he's traveling

with Jane Hart. I was just wondering if you knew where they might go. I was told she had a home at Joshua Tree."

"She sold her house. She needed the money. I always told her, someday she'd wind up like the rest of us. She'd run outa places. She can't do flicks the way I could. She doesn't have the body for it. Randall's too young for her. Getting pregnant by him was crazy. All he's good for is to listen to music and watch TV, talk about people Janey knew, live in a community house and take meals in a hall."

"They have a house at the edge of the forest off Keller."

"It won't last. She won't be able to hang onto it. Neither will he. Even if he inherits he's too young to know what to do with it."

"You think he had his old man killed?"

"You gotta be kidding. Geneva set him up. You watch. When they read the will, it'll be her or his assistant King who walks off with the sling. Probably her. They'll probably make Randall wait ten years."

"There's a first wife."

"I know, but face it, she's got her own money and plenty of it from what I hear. It's not Wes' to begin with. Title was never deeded over. Just because it was a forest one day and a suburb fifty years later doesn't mean anything was done the way it shoulda been. Without Geneva, Milt woulda kept his shares and mosta the land woulda stayed in his family."

"Can anyone prove your story?"

"Milt coulda, but he's little more than a vegetable."

I drove to Oakland's County Assessor. I came across the Hauptman deed along with fifteen other deeds and names of men and a woman who shared tenement rights under the Peralta and Patterson tracts which made up the forty thousand acres from Santa Clara to Calaveras. The land was described in a note that read, To Horwith Barrows, Esq., Attorney of Association Territory. Dear Sir — As concerns the governance of Brooklyn Township from the southernmost creekbed which begins at the Hayward Bay and empties inland at Meadowes to the easterly point on the Carquinez Strait to the north to Calaveras, the land rights are conveniently shared by Handley Cabrilla, C. Cobb, Johnathan Cousins, Marchand Domingues, Padilla Goma, Roberto Leandro, Stephen Mandeville, Captain Adam Montgomery, Lieutenant Lawrence O'Donald, William Quareles, Estrella don Salvador, Michael Redding, Josephina Vallejo. The late tragedy which befell the village town situated on Adeline when on June 16, 1878 the contemptible act by Mr. Cousins' son did fire upon his fellow countrymen causing bloodshed and grave mutilation. The Court of Sessions ordered the remedy as a transfer of ownership to the father Johnathan Cousins, enlarging his share to three hundred acres along Hayward Creek. This will not censure the family but shall make restitution in a responsible manner. Signed: Sonoma, William B. Ide, Governor, September 14, 1878.

In another skirmish following the death of Jonathan Cousins, who had no surviving heir, the County Recorder found: On January 30, 1904 there occurred a shooting fatality by Cobb of Sonya Wilson, wife of Denver Wilson, for her breaking off a treatise. At the preliminary hearing by the Justice of the Peace a verdict of self-defense was recorded. Bail was posted at two hundred dollars. Based upon evidence put forth however, it appears that Cobb in haste went to the Wilson home where he stormed through the house and finding Sonya in the room with her two children did shoot her in the chest. He turned himself into the Constable later that day. This violent act and cost to the Wilson home was fined at six hundred dollars. This amount was seized by the State in the form of a hundred acres.

CHAPTER 19.

"**THEY THINK** they've located him."

Teresa D'Coteur stood in her doorway. She seemed more possessed than she had in a long time. Her bearing, sybaritic under less stressful circumstances, was self consciously taut with anticipation. If she to this day assessed criminal disposition in a career as an attorney, she could absent herself in any way the situation might require.

I caught her around the waist. "Let's go inside," I urged.

We stepped inside the cool interior of the house. On all sides glass looked onto separate patios and the garden. The temperament of our lives which had been seeded and reseeded into winter and summer places of contentment had been altered by the unforeseen.

"He called. I thought I'd never hear from him again." Her voice was tearful, bordering on gratitude. "He agreed to come to wherever you want. "

I sat and she did the same on the adjacent sofa. The couches were upholstered white silk with dark teak cane. The lamp tables were also a dark teak and long in carved elegance. She began at the beginning. Randall had called her from an undisclosed area. He had fled with Hart from a man's home in the desert after taking a file from his safe. He shouldn't have looked but the file contained names he knew. He had sense enough to know that his knowledge of their existence in relation to the job he'd been asked to do could get him killed.

"They left before dawn," she recapped. "He said they headed for the mountains and were planning on getting a plane out of the state. Randall has a pilot friend who flies surgical materials to Reno and Seattle. He said if you could meet him out of the state — "

"Did he say where?" I asked her.

"Oregon, Washington. He said he could arrange to give you whatever he has. He said he was sorry for all the trouble he's caused. He said something about Bolivar not being the problem. He was insistent that you should know this."

"Terry, you know Randall better than any of us. To whom would he go? Where would he stay?"

"It must be one of Hart's friends. He doesn't know anyone up there."

"Not if these are Hart's connections. They'd be running from these people, not to them."

She conceded with a nod. "He used to ask why Wes brought in so many contingency firms when he had a company who did top notch security. Wes always said in a split second if a hacker grabbed onto your page, you had to have diversion as well as a second entry. People who hopefully weren't well known who could go in and scan the break-in for information. He'll go for one of those firms with local technicians." She was giddy, or not putting two and two together.

"It doesn't sound right," I said soberly to slow her down. "Why don't you think he's seeking as many backup systems as he can find to eliminate problems for a job?"

"Don't do this to me, Lenn. He's my son. I'm all he's got."

"But this is not the Randall you know. If he's gone to so much trouble to first define the parameters of local security, then went to Professor Ames, now has taken a file — that's alot of trouble. He's doing this for a reason."

"Why don't you meet with him? Hear what he has to say?"

"I'm not sure I want to, Terry. What kind of job requires me to leave the state?"

That point sunk in. "Why would he bring in people for this?" Terry asked, wondering aloud.

"I have no idea, except that it must be the problem Wes was having keeping these hackers out."

"The ruby display is the next best thing to a failsafe system," Terry replied. "Wes paid a mint for it. Even if his database vanishes he can still target the paintings by an outside system and re-engage the alarm."

"What is the most expensive item the system protects?"

"The diamond of course. It is equipped with a security system that is virtually impenetrable. Once you're in the building you can't get out."

"Why did he feel he needed this type of system?"

"The feds felt he needed it. When he went to his backup system it was down also. What he believed was adequately protected by satellite was inconsistently veiled. He became concerned. Not only that, but the museum is located in San Francisco which faces the ocean, and there is nothing between it and Golden Gate Park. If this lineup can be penetrated by a system in a park, it can be penetrated virtually anywhere."

I gave this some thought. There had been a string of break-ins which confused a system that already had sophisticated entry.

"There were more than five break-ins," she said, as if reading my mind. "The fact was these hackers were exceptional. They reversed the tape, causing the guards to view all rooms and paintings backwards. They also taped over pre-recorded tape making the final tape appear staggered. The consultant team he brought in felt the hacks were designed to provide an interior map such that if a heist were to be pulled, all egress routes would be disabled for at least ten hours. His concern was that with a bank on the ground floor, a restaurant on the second, a gallery of prize items on the third floor, on the fourth the archives and on the fifth the museum, he was vulnerable. Because of this he redesigned the placement of doors, had some open into blind corridors.

"I remember I used to keep thinking, whose access was eliminated by the introduction of this system. I thought it could be a collector. I thought it was someone we knew or worse, someone Mitchel Hauptman knew. His son was killed and for all anyone knows it was over this. It was around that time Wes bought the system. Now Wes is dead. A million dollars is gone. They've probably put Randall on ice in some fashion."

"I think it's Hart."

"I didn't realize you thought that about her."

"Yes, I do. These people are very serious contenders for a heist of this system right now, today. I believe it's for a job they intend to pull. It's expensive to invade a system just to prove you can get in. There has to be a stronger motivation. Try the diamond, for instance."

"You have easily a dozen collections. Losing these could wreak havoc on the museum's reputation, not to mention cost hundreds of millions of dollars."

"I agree. But it's not practical to think a group of thieves are going to waltz out with a hundred paintings. In tossing them down the chute, some would be damaged. It wouldn't be worth the trouble. A stunning diamond the size of your fingernail and small enough to pocket is the item."

She said, "No way to get to it. The roof is glass, there is one entry to the room, that entry is monitored around the clock — there's just no way, Lenn."

I eyed the room. It was pleasant, simple with macrame wall hangings and oil paintings of still life — an orange, a bowl of strawberries which I recognized was an Averty, an Aloe Vera plant on a table with a white tablecloth; a room for sipping tea and enjoying a garden in bloom. Azaleas, sweet pea, a train of nightshade, slate stones on gravel, a haphazard bush of pink roses climbing a fence, lent itself to a touch of wildness amidst a conservative look, enhancing the effect of the sitting room.

I said, "He's a high school dropout with a baby. At some point he's going to need some serious money. If he's already burned his bridges, and he thinks he might not collect on his father's will, then this act would be insurance for him."

She wore a momentary shield of quiet, a habit which over time I had learned to respect. Her brooding was less self reflective than a respite to detach from her desire to defend against me. Finally she said, "I'm aware this situation is not nice. If the security is breached, it isn't as if it affects the bank. It is after all a museum."

"Did my mother tell you about the mess I'm in?"

Randall's voice sharply pierced the air with a twang of resentment.

"She did say you might need a ride home."

"I can't leave, Lenn. I'm stuck. I was in an accident and as a result I can't walk."

"How about I arrange for medical care at Evergreen?"

"I'm not there. Jane went on ahead, but I developed a bad leg after the accident and moving puts me in agony."

"Where are you?"

"Trojan Park. Janey knows someone with a cabin here. It was our plan to spend the remainder of the spring and summer together."

It was a long time to hole up. I had the feeling that if I didn't fly in, I might not see Randall again. This was a goodbye. "When was she going to pull the job, Randall?"

"The stone is gone, Lenn. We pulled the job a week ago when Adam went to the Hyatt."

I felt myself tremble with anger. I didn't know which affected me more — wanting to deny this petulant young man any sense of dignity or wanting to find a way to damn him to hell. "Your father was murdered, you goddamn cocksucker."

Randall went on, speaking as if more out of a need to clear the air, "It's not a big deal, you know. Everything's insured. It's not like any of us would be putting this on our resume."

"Did you hear me?"

"Dad accused me of jamming the system. He said he was going to put a codicil into effect. As usual he was being a fucking stupid ass," Randall said, in the easy tone of one who comes to feel all is justified because the crime was there for the taking and could be taken. "All you have to do is close one entry to shut down the system. Oh, don't sweat it, Lenn. I know what you're thinking. That it was callous of me — "

"Didn't you hear what I said?"

"I heard you," Randall said stonily. "You said my dad died. I'm not sorry, you know. I didn't have friends before Janey came along. Living with Gen and my dad was hell. Half the time they didn't notice me."

"Quit the talk. Try having a reaction."

"Well, I didn't kill him. Is that what you're asking me, Lenn? If I had anything to do with it? There's tens of people who didn't like him, who thought he was unfair, selfish, bigoted."

"Have some remorse, Randall. I don't want to bring you home and expose your mother to this garbage."

"It won't matter your coming here. I can't move. When I try to stand it all but slips out from under. Look, if it's any help I wasn't a good enough son. I knew it. So did he. Some things, once they're done, that's it. You can't change them. He didn't want me around. What was I s'posed to do? I was always trying to get his attention, but he wasn't around to get it from. I had to face reality, didn't I? I had to come to terms that I was in the way." He was crying. "I'm only seventeen. There aren't many places that accept you if you're under age. What was I supposed to do? I mean, damn it, Lenn, he didn't want to be a father, at least not to me."

"I'm on my way, Randall. Stay put, okay?"

"Okay." His body wracked with sobs. "The job was already underway. I didn't do much. Janey had a friend who was going to get us out of town, a lady by name of Vera Stranger, but she didn't come through. At the last minute, Janey said Stranger didn't show. Janey even went to her home but no one was there."

The case had melted in the rain. "I'll be there in about five hours."

"I'm not going nowhere. I killed my leg. I can't do anything but drag it around like a crutch."

I didn't tell Terry where I was going. I didn't tell her what her son had revealed. It would undo her, kill off the remaining adoration she felt for him.

Greed was a terrible thing. So was envy. I didn't know which was worse — which robbed the spirit more. The desire to possess sudden wealth, to rise above the commonplace, to not have to work, to not be worn by stress could come at a great price. Both emotions caused many teens, not to mention adults, to travel paths they ought not to. For a youth like Randall, bereft of friendship and parental support, it cast him to sea, separating him from the values of his upbringing.

There was snow on the ground when I flew into Sea Tac Airport in Seattle. It was a fluke of nature — for summer. Snow had swept the surrounding foothills a dark blue.

I rented a sedan. At four o'clock in the afternoon, the drive to Trojan Park was a good three hours. Once I departed the busy streets of congested traffic, stone mansions and five story condominium complexes in and around the upscale warehouse district that sat on the waterfront, the highway shot beneath a series of looping freeways and steel framed bridges. Past large signs overhead, I sped into back country. The forests were gone, replaced by industry, life at a minimalistic presentation. The river looked as though if one could see to a mud or silt bottom, the mud would be yellowish brown.

The aspen in marshy fields were thin, crowded, like tall pitchforks. Through the dense foliage it looked as if cement had turned to a rich dark shale scaling down some two to three hundred feet. The air was bleak and cold. Red and natural brown farmhouses sporadically lined a field of cut grass where cows grazed. A recent rain had caused this particular field to become saturated with nowhere for the water to go. A railroad wended through clusters of fir and ferns and through aspen groves, their long sleek white trunks elegant and virtuous. Past small towns signs pointed to the State Department of Forestry. Here and there were blond wood, long houses — light colored brown shingle, very neat, Scandanavian construction, like rows of bird houses.

Out of a leafy wilderness the nuclear power museum shaped like an L, Trojan Park loomed into the open. A lake fronted the Visitor Center and observatory. I turned down the one lane road that led to a house which was designated City Hall at the corner of School and Neely Streets. Numerous houses were boarded up. It was the impoverished look of single story, darkly wooden cabins surrounded by densely cloaked redwoods that told me a person could die out here unnoticed. I parked and walked up the stairs to the one house where a red van was parked.

"I'm looking for a young man by name of Randall Roark," I told the man in the wheelchair who opened the door. The man was in his thirties, with straight reddish hair to the shoulders, a checkered flannel shirt and jeans and workman's boots.

"He has a bad leg." I added.

"Oh rightio. Janey's friend. They've got him at the infirmary. You know, he's not going to walk out of here."

"Why not?"

"Abscess. We see alot of that around here. This is logging country. May be California's industry got shot to hell, but we still log 'em here round the clock. Most common problem is frostbite."

"Thanks," I said, feeling disconcerted, and cautiously stepped down off the porch.

I walked the block to the infirmary. Flickering through the trees was the river, and an enclosed harbor with a sound wall, jetty of rocks, pier, storm barrier and small fishing boats with pulleys on them, moving slow coming in at four knots.

The man who answered was obviously Jane Hart's relation. He was roughly her age, in his early to mid thirties, red short hair, fair complected, blue eyed, very angular, thin boned especially through the arms and wrists. "Name's Ferd. Roger Ferd."

We shook hands.

Through a narrow hall that was damp and smelled of the salty ocean, Roger led me into a room at the back of the house that was nearly all windows and faced the river. On a bed of old style Norwegian white and navy blue quilts lay Randall. Roger grunted something inaudible and left the two of us alone.

"You look well," I said, and took a rattan armchair beside the bed. I eyed the teenager. He wore baggy trousers with a large, white flannel shirt underneath suspenders and white socks with red tops. "I expected you to be in much worse shape." I said.

"Well," Randall said in a jocular tone faintly reminiscent of his father, "I am about as poorly as one can be considering I can't walk."

"The man up the street said you have an abscess."

Randall rolled his leggings up over his left leg to reveal what appeared to be a fresh wound on his leg the size of a fist. "Roger's sent for the physician at Astoria to come down. He was supposed to come this afternoon but he was detained at Portland."

"Will Jane be joining you?"

"Soon, soon. She had to shop for the baby. So, you don't think much of me, Lenn, do you?"

"I'm disappointed. You'll have to face charges once you cross state lines."

"I'm not going back, old girl. Dad promised to cut me out. He said he'd ditch me entirely after what I'd done. I didn't think it was fair, but it's his money. He was going to leave it all to Genieve."

"Do you know what caused his decision?"

"Love, I guess. He didn't tell me."

"What was he under the impression you had done?"

"Offed Hauptman, I guess."

"Did you?"

Randall shook his head. He was an adult now, his expression and combined rancor clearly connoted that. Ash curly hair, longish, manly posture, slack jaw. "I broke into Knowles' system. It was easy. The dude had everything coming in. I found a guy in the delta who said he had a buyer for the whole damned lot."

"Any possibility the person you nixed out of the deal was Genieve?"

"That'd be a fucking scream, Lenn. Nothing could be funnier."

"She was Knowles' wife."

"I never met his wife."

I stared him down. He was a stupid, naive prick who deserved no less than a prison cell. "What did your dad do, to turn you into an instrument of betrayal?"

"I found a document draft. I'm the one who was betrayed, Lenn. I'm the one. I have to say I was dumbfounded. As usual he had no explanation. Sat there, stoney, non committal."

"He must have had said something to you."

"All he said was, it's not signed yet."

"Any possibility he knew you were involved in a scheme to bilk him?"

"Oh, that's a good one!"

"It's the timing of your actions, Randall."

"Well, why the hell shouldn't I inherit? I mean, hello. That was meant to be my money by age twenty-five."

"Maybe he didn't intend to sign; maybe he was thinking it over."

"Well, who would've killed him? Genieve? She married him with a fortune in tow."

"I was told she had none."

"No, she owned an adjoining two hundred acres."

"That's not alot. I understand her family once owned the land trust now held by your father. It used to be fifty thousand acres."

"I know, but it's gone."

"Did you talk to him about breaking the will?"

"I tried to. I told him he couldn't just cut me out. He said the problem was it wasn't a forest anymore because the plots that had been forested land now had houses on them. I went to the county offices and looked up the original parcels. In 1897 Geneva's great grandparents owned a fifty thousand acre tract which they lost through some quirk of fate twenty years before my father purchased his acreage from the county. My dad said as late as 1955 the land was forest, albeit deeded to the county. There were any number of recorded land disputes. He said if I walked the matter into a court of law, my chances were fifty-fifty, a decision would be found against me and I'd lose his current shares of land."

"You went to alot of trouble with this."

"Janey said I had a right to inherit. You would've said so."

"But you've committed a crime. You can't hope to inherit now."

"I'm not worried about it. I'll get money for the friggin' diamond."

"But you have to get it first."

Randall cast an all knowing glance. A glance that said he was smarter than his father, smarter than I, than any of us.

I eyed him. "Why don't you start over? How did you get in?"

"The way anyone gets in. Through the front door. You can't worry that the security camera sees you. That's part of the work. We went in dressed in blue coveralls and face guards a half hour before the doors were to open. Although security had us on the spools we had a good fifteen minutes before anyone would show. We 4-armed the display. One man drilled the bolt that holds the glass display in place while we shut off the light system surrounding the diamond and one guy lifted the glass to remove it. Once we were done we disrobed to our street wear and left the coverall suits on the floor."

"How did you arrive?"

"By muni."

"Well, you didn't just cart the diamond around with you on the subway?"

"We hired in a delivery truck and we shoved the stone into a baggie into the gas tank. Then we cut a hole in the tank and transferred to a VW. The driver took the car to his home, put the stone in a jar with paste and then left the door open for the fence. Within twenty-four hours the stone was on its way and we had a cool ten million to split between us."

"How many are you?"

"Just five. That includes the women to case the building, the Bolivars who set up the heist, the fence and then us to pull the heist." He grinned. "It's not as though we took everything. We've done thefts of drawers. Normally we take two to three sections which yield fifty or so diamonds and take a pouch of cutting stones. You need the cutting stones to make your getaway otherwise you can be tracked in a day. Don't ask me why. Jane could probably tell you. But for my dad's, we just raided the fifth floor, took his diamond and then pulled the pulley out of the casing in the elevator in making our getaway."

I was in a state of shock. "What about that ransom? Wouldn't that have been enough?"

"Janey said that was necessary to figure out what kind of security we might have to penetrate. As it turned out, once I opened the gates and jammed the circuits, all the man who the Bolivars had take the money had to do was walk in and remove the son of a bitch briefcase."

So many details for a young man. Wouldn't it have been easier to accept the blow of fate and take a high paid desk job in his father's company?

Roger brought in two cups of hot coffee on a tray with cream and sugar cubes.

"Is it possible to move him?" I asked.

"He can't walk on that leg, Ms. Cliford. If he tries to stand, you'll see what I mean. Dinner will be served in the dining room in a half hour." He departed from the room, turning on the overhead light as he left.

"In a day you'll hate me, Lenn. I can feel that cold wind coming on. It's a bear, but I'm not going to let any dog catcher catch this dog."

We sat for a moment without speaking. Randall poured cream and dropped several cubes of brown sugar into his porcelain cup and slowly sipped. I took mine black with sugar. The issues of the day would have to be dealt with another hour. Reckoning and figuring out how to make amends would not come easily but I was fairly certain Randall knew the name and identifying information of the fence and appraiser. There were few dealers who would chase after such a stone in such a brazen way.

Finally Randall said, "How did he die?"

"He was shot at point blank range."

"You must be kidding." Then: "That's not possible. She promised it wouldn't be like that."

"Who? Janey?" A second later I realized he was attempting to make his own getaway. "No one was in the house when it occurred. Your father had sent Adam home. Your stepmother was out."

Randall looked sickly. "I didn't kill him."

"I'm going to be blunt, Randall. Why did you hang around Jane if you knew what she was after?"

"I just wanted to take a stab at him. Then after the ransom, when we knew if we acted within that same hour we could pull it off, the anger sort of went away. When I found him inside the house, not where he should be — "

"What do you mean? When did you find him at the house?"

"He was supposed to make that drop. Yas said it'd be a cinch. He had this friend Vera who could do anything with a lock. He said he'd send her to get the combination. Everyone would do a different task. That way nothing could be pinned on any one person. I was to open the safe from the house using the pegs as guides for where to pull the page handle bar on the database. Yas would send this lackey in to pick up the goods from the transfer and that would be that.

"But when I arrived at the house, my father was waiting for me. He said, here's the money. It won't last a year at the rate you're going. I said, fuck off, I won't take your damned money. He said, I'm leaving it on my desk. If you want it, it's right there. I didn't take it. I figured he probably had that purple stuff that comes off on your hands all over the bills. I went to my room, did my thing and left."

"I don't believe you. You or someone else took the money, and you turned off the cameras to do it. Is it here?"

"What do you take me for? Stupid?"

I'd never say to his face what I thought of him now. He was little better than a damned terrorist.

A road that led past a group of warehouses was gated and locked with a chain.

In the foreground alongside the buoy sat a large yacht, its large blue sails the size of masts, its broad wooden deck making for about forty-seven feet of boat. Below would be the kitchen, bed and bathroom, barely enough space for two.

Near the shore rested a houseboat with two men, tall in white rain gear and long boots, fishing off the bow, an eye on the yacht.

I watched as one man, small, presumably African or possibly Australian, hard to tell at a distance, waited on deck, his long black shirt rippling in a wind. In a rowboat his companion, an equally short narrow framed man, came toward the dock. This would be the jewel appraiser who came from Johannesburg direct whom the man at the Saturday Marketplace told me to expect.

The man who tied up the dinghy and climbed the wooden trellis to the dock was four feet nine inches. His walk was quick, trim, vigorous. In his hand he carried a satchel. He nodded to me as we entered a door of a house attached to a warehouse beneath the entanglement of freeways on the shipping side of Seattle.

Once inside he switched on a light. In the middle of a homey kitchen with throw rugs everywhere was a wooden table and chairs. Through a hall I could see into a room with fiberglass kayaks sledded onto rafters. We sat at the table. The man withdrew a scale, pen, pad and ink and small case. From the case he withdrew a pinkish white stone the rumored size of the Berlin taken from the Roark Museum. He handed me a glass and the stone.

I squinted at the stone. It appeared flawless but for one slanting cut, its dimensions deep, bevelled and smooth. "It's a cutting stone."

"It is the companion stone that is wanted, stolen by his son. It is believed to have been fenced by a team of nurses. Gone also was the seal written in Arabic that was considered text for the stone."

"How is that useful?"

"Well these are holograms. The stone appears as a hologram within the text which is always in the safe room of the building where the stone is housed. A trade secret," he said, with a wink.

"Who was the fence? Do you know?"

"A woman named Jane Hart. The buyer, I believe, is the person you want to speak to."

❖ ❖ ❖

Bookshelves crammed with intellectual sounding titles lined one wall. Books I knew — Tristes Tropiques, Men and Masculinity, A Book of Men — caught my eye. On the walls were French opera masks by Inigo Jones and a scrolled sonnet by Ben Johnson. Bevelled glass like Austrian crystal captured sunlight in a prism separating light into colors of the rainbow which slanted over the large black square of a Berber rug centered on a blonde hardwood floor.

"Well, Ms. Cliford, what can we do for you?" The speaker was female, five foot eight with panels of black hair that hung on either side of her smooth face. She wore a dark red A-line skirt with a silk cream colored top on her sensuous body.

"Facsimile and stone," I said.

"Please."

I followed her into a large, elongated sitting room which overlooked a hothouse garden of ferns and leafy palms, oriental lilies. We sat on white silk couches. Glass tables, dark cherry wood vases and elephant carved lamps with dark red shades tastefully filled the room.

"All diamonds are accompanied by some kind of document," she said, with consideration to introduce me to the idea of museum-valued jewels. "Topaki, Star of Egypt — the Nile — the Pink Panther — all stunningly perfect jewels each valued at a million minimum. This jewel is worth at least ninety million."

"Do you know anything about its history of ownership?"

"Yes, it has had two owners. The first permitted it to be displayed at the Louvre and the second, Wesley Roark, purchased it from Warefeld and Rich who just happens to be American. Its corresponding seal had the company's initials embossed into its cover. Mr. Roark, I am told, was amused by the fact that the initials were the same as his."

"Have you seen these items?"

"Not yet. I am assuming they will be delivered to the party by midday."

"And when they are?"

"I do not fool myself into thinking this principal has gone to such trouble and expense to turn the items over to an insurance agent or return it to the museum. This has been a brutal outcome already. No one anticipated there would be human life spilled."

"Might I know your principal?" I asked, but I thought I already knew. This was either a program of greed or of consumerism, not of vengeance, of rightfulness.

She tilted her head slightly, and balked. "I can't do that. I'm sorry. I will say only that the buyer is not the actual interest."

She removed a diamond taking a tweezer like instrument and held it over a small light. "See how the rock shines? Absolutely brilliant. It's worth more than Topaki."

I marveled at the glints in the stone which shone in a multitudinous glow of perfection. "I can assure you this is the cut Berlin stone. "

"Where is its twin?"

"Ah, the buyer has it."

20. SAN FRANCISCO

AS I SAT IN THE DARK and listened to the almost inaudible cutting sounds made by the individual dressed in dark ski wear positioned on the roof like a cat, I considered the situation for the woman who had made her reputation by climbing down a rope. She was washed up. Not so her husband who had choreographed a dance for fifty people into the Louvre. That man, wherever he was at this very moment, had an equally effective understudy.

A coarse wind emanated from the apex where red lights glowed in the night. As he steadied the pane on top of the glass roof and lowered a single steel cable into the room, I wondered why he needed to do this at all, why he didn't simply walk into the museum with a team of fifty people and take the diamond off its pedestal. It had to be that the ruby paintings — the line-up of six abstract paintings — were capable of somehow disabling a group. I heard the metal box attach to the roof rendering the cable taut with tension. The individual lowered himself down the cable, keeping his legs also rigid. He moved quickly, quietly, his entire body and face sheathed in dark clothing, everything except his hands. He made it down the cable in less than a minute, then attached a magnet to the glass display and raised the glass like a trap door for a mouse. He swiped the diamond in exchange for a bevelled pyramid made from a prism and released the magnet. He hoisted himself up the steel cable, his hands and arms taking his weight until he was to the top. Then he snapped the cable into the box. Next he placed the cut glass pane back into place and epoxied the edges. He had another fifteen seconds to go before the alarm would go off. The moment he picked up the cable box, the proprietor switched on the lights.

❖ ❖ ❖

We ran down the glade below clusters of trees. In the distance the crashing sounds of waves against the beach could be heard. The cat burglar was no longer carrying the cable box. He was moving rapidly, his thin body operating with steely precision through the park. Police vehicles had joined the chase, their sirens silent, red light flashing in long strides, their lights flooding the street.

A helicopter hovered overhead shining a hall of light onto the street. The man reversed his direction and the overhead spotlight leapt in front of him. He reversed like a caged animal, then jumped into the street and was immediately hit hard by an advancing police car. We ran into the street to surround the fallen man. The officer had left his motor running and his door open. He knelt beside the frozen man on the pavement. With one hand on his gun, he pulled back the ski hood to reveal the man's head.

"Well, I'll be goddamned," he said, about the blond man's face. "It's Milt Cousins, Gabi's ex."

"Small world," I said. "Who is he to you?"

"He's a cop, Lady. San Francisco P.D. from way back when. He retired after his son took a fall in a road accident. It was one of our biggest cases. There was a collision with a truck carrying windows for a job at the Basin. More glass than you dreamed possible. It was everywhere."

"He's in the diamond trade."

"I can see that. At the time, it was his case. He equipped warehouses with flight recorder boxes. No one could figure how the hell the crates were stolen without the boxes picking up the information." He rifled through Cousins' pockets until he found the diamond. "Look at this, will you?" He held the jewel in the palm of his hand.

"It's worth a fortune," I said.

The proprietor stood beside me. "It's worth more than money. It's worth blood."

Chapter 21. Oakland

THEY WERE CAREFUL, morbidly so. The facsimile would be delivered to its awaiting owner and the jewel transported at some future date, perhaps giving the buyer time to admire the conquest. And then because these details were merely means to an end, a loan would be taken out on the new value of the stolen jewel and negotiations entered into by midnight of the first working day of the next business week.

In reality it was a smart move to make. It was the single piece of collateral that one was capable of utilizing to back the economy of the future enterprises that made up the entire Roark conglomerate.

Even the attorney could not have had so much at stake. This had to be the swift unerring move on a human chessboard on which Wall Street could not be relied upon to recreate a financially sound partnership. Aside from Terry who had real ties, despite what would someday be seen as tragic failing of her young son, only Genieve stood to inherit any substance. But apart from cash and liquid assets, without a bank or groupings of title companies, the money would be spent down within twenty years or less. The Bolivars would exit under the flurry of stadium heists and a ransom, and poor Randall would spend his adulthood wondering how he could have been so easily led astray. Hauptman too would shrink with Jones and a handful of other wannabe superstar diamond owners, Stranger among them. I thought it was regrettable that Hart, to whom all catheters and lifelines clung, had to know who the principal was.

There were some crimes whose duplicity was seldom if ever palpated. Crimes which relied upon each party — from fence to doer of deed and subsequent diversionary acts — had no way to know who pulled the strings for any subsequent act, thus freeing its parties to act without fear of exposure or of getting caught.

As I sat in the shadows of a wooded overhang, the burst of plumeria mingled with the stuffy scent of bougainvillea. Diffuse light cast impressions of dappled patterns on the road. The slow green jaguar crept up the road, its windshield a lively reflection of leaves and sunlight. I turned on my engine and took my time as I followed the Jaguar up to Parnassus Drive onto the Roark estate.

Genieve did not see me straightaway. She stepped out of the car, her medium thin frame presented elegantly in a black suit and matching pumps. She reached for the trunk and froze as I parked behind her.

I smiled and she did also.

"Mrs. Roark."

"Ms. Cliford."

I opened the trunk and seeing two secured metal carrying containers took them and waited for her to take out her key.

"Am I under arrest?" she asked.

"It depends what is inside these."

She gave a deprecating nod. "Yes, I suppose it does."

She walked swiftly, resigned now to putting up appearances. She walked up the marble stairs, opened the door and stepped aside to let me pass.

"In we go," I said. "After you."

"After me," she echoed, and entered the cool temperature of the marble foyer and hall. She led into the living room and placed each valise on the glass table.

I sat opposite her. I snapped open the first case and found a safe. I gently snapped the lid closed and eyed her.

"Do you have the combination?"

She spun the dial, two notches to the right, five past it to the left, one to the right. The door released. Inside, mounted on a black velvet throne sat the other half of the Berlin diamond, inside glass, about the size of a woman's pinky nail. The hologram behind it looked as if it could match the original stone.

"Gen?" Sylvan Reese entered through the hall. "Darling?" And stopped in his tracks. "Might I know what brings you here, Ms. Cliford?"

I stood, and opened my cell phone. "Backup should arrive within the next few minutes."

She was sullen as she stood to greet her late husband's solicitor. "Van," was all she had time to say.

"What the hell do you mean, what took so long?" Shouted an excited lead detective from the Oakland Police Department who was standing in for Detective Brice. "It's not as if we got lost. We know our way."

"We got lost," the fingerprint woman acknowledged. She was a brunette in her coiffed hairdo. "The deputy always complains when he has to come up here. He says the streets are like false doors and once here, you aren't meant to leave."

"That's why there are so few burglaries."

"Or the burglars live here."

Behind her, an insurance agent squeezed inside the hall. She stood head and shoulders above the other police officers and crime scene technicians, long red wavy hair, blue eyes, an alert detail-driven investigator who did not shy away from any heist. "Hey, Lenn," she yelled and waved.

I waved in response. "Rob. You see the two out front?"

"Wife and esquire? In the paddy wagon, I saw. She's put on dark glasses. I've been expecting this a long time. Her husband had a few items walk out of here with no clear sign as to what occurred."

"Goods are on the table. You'll like the diamonds."

I watched as Rob unscrewed the box out of the carrying

container and placed it into a briefcase. "What will you prosecute for?"

"Maximum sentence. We'll get it too. These folks should've known better, especially the attorney. Can you imagine?"

The ability to house a diamond could only have come with the series of intrusions that lay scattered in a neighbors yard. "Looks like she hired in Hart."

"No kidding. Her family would've inherited the other half of Oakland back in 1953 or whenever the hell it was if not for that shooting death at the OK Corral. There's a long history to this."

"Any idea when you'll want to interview me?"

"Go home. I'll call when I'm done processing all this paperwork."

I said. "Tonight I'll be at the home of the first wife if you need me."

"Okay. Take care, Lenn."

"Will do." As I inched through the hall, I thought what a tragedy it was that Roark had died. He was a good man, the last in a long line of southern gents whose money paid to clear forests and resurrect cities from smaller villages, stables and crossings.

Marion nailed his hat on the sofa, circled an arm around my waist.

"Nice to see you, Mom," he said. "I brought my dog."

"I didn't know you had a dog, Sweetheart."

"Yeah, I just bought her." The dog turned out to be a terrier and was sleek and blonde. "Pretty, huh?"

"Beautiful. What's her name?"

"Big dog."

"How are you, Big dog?" I teased the dog and took out a beef bone from the refrigerator and set it on the floor."

"Hey, Mom, that's swell. You happy, old blubber?"

"Did you bring your girlfriend?"

"Nope. Rehearsals this week and next. It's a wretched schedule. I wish to God Mari was home more but this drama stuff is her first love. Not me — you're my first love."

I nicked him on the side of the chin. "It's never too late to reconsider."

He poured glasses of wine and handed me one. "Want to take a few pictures?" He threw me a tiny digital camera.

We posed in front of the grill, happy as clams. Marion draped his arm over my shoulders, this hulking lad who stood almost four inches over me, cheery and affectionate, genuine and humorous. I took the photo shots. Marion hugged me tightly to him, causing me for an instant to feel wistful. I had grown up with the sense that I fit somewhere else, not in my milieu and was often asking, should I be here, or there? It never occurred to me that if I took out a map I would see my place in the world straight away, that I would be able to say, ah, I'm from here. My parents after all, although they looked Scottish said they were Russian, and because I was a trusting sort brought up to believe things were only as they represented them to be, I did not inquire, even though I was frequently struck by oddities that told me there was another reality separate from the one I was familiar with. So I gave my son as much sameness as I could, baseball and soccer twice a week each up to age ten and guitar lessons on weekends along with a tutor from eleven to thirteen. I gave him an organic, predominantly vegetarian meal plan and fed him nighttime stories such that he'd be fascinated by the world around him but sought to provide him with a base of emotional security, one that could be governed by spontaneity, not just by yearnings for a life one suspected might be out there. And here he was, and as he beamed at me I could tell he was filled with a desire to contain every last bounty, with no need to belong to it, free somehow in a way I wasn't.